PRAISE FOR
CURSE OF THE KLONDIKE

"Set amid the Klondike Gold Rush of the late 1800s, *Curse of the Klondike* is a literary treat for lovers of historical western fiction and readers who fancy rough-around-the edges and colorful characters facing challenges we can only imagine today. The narrative constantly tempts the reader to mine the depths of twists and turns to glean whether fate, retribution for past lives› sins, rotten-to-the-core genes, or divine intervention, explains recurring hardship and tragedy and crime. Borrowing from his work as a poet, Rick Taylor takes readers by the hand on a searing and seamless excursion through history that will make your head shake."

—Michael J. Coffino, award-winning author of
Truth Is in the House

"Curse of the Klondike is a crisply written, imagery-packed book that takes readers along for a ride that spans generations. Rick Taylor has produced a gripping story about love, adventure, tragedy, redemption, and a perilous curse that must be confronted before it can be conquered. It's compelling from start to finish."

—Ken Gormley, President of Duquesne University and
New York Times bestselling author

"As a long-time fan of Rick Taylor's poetry, I was eager to read his first full-length novel, *Curse of the Klondike*. Not surprisingly, he transitioned genres with great finesse, masterfully incorporating quirky and humorous poems into a rich, compelling, and totally satisfying adventure."

—Alan B. Gibson, retired advertising executive
and current author

"*Curse of the Klondike* is a fast-paced adventure of three generations of one family, beginning with Shorty Shaw's escape from the Great fire of San Francisco and his misadventures in the Klondike Gold Rush. Against the backdrop of American history, Taylor traces the destructive effects of bi-polar disease—little understood by those who suffered from it as well as those they encountered. His saga is a gripping tale of endurance, love, and redemption."

—Sara Smith, retired Emeritus Professor of English at
Montgomery College

"*Curse of the Klondike* blends historic events with the story in a very interesting way. It would make a great movie."

—Betty Snyder, author of *Born but Not Buried* and
The Truest Color

Curse of the Klondike: A Misadventure Novel
by Rick Taylor

© Copyright 2022 Rick Taylor

ISBN 978-1-64663-814-7

Published by

 köehlerbooks™

3705 Shore Drive
Virginia Beach, VA 23455
800-435-4811
www.koehlerbooks.com

Curse
of the
Klondike

A Misadventure Novel

Rick Taylor

VIRGINIA BEACH
CAPE CHARLES

To my wife Shannon, my Pixie from Texas

A PIXIE FROM TEXAS
She has captured my soul
this pixie from Texas
this enchantress
whose smile
always lifts me high
offering proof of her generosity
and caring.

I'm blessed
that she has chosen me
a struggling writer and poet
whose light has yet to shine.
Who can doubt
that her love and brilliance
will charge my engines
and change my water
into wine.

THE SPELL OF THE YUKON
by Robert W. Service

I wanted the gold and I sought it.
I scrabbled and mucked like a slave.
Was it famine or scurvy, I found it;
I hurled my youth into the grave.
I wanted the gold and I got it—
Came out with a fortune last fall—
Yet somehow life's not what I thought it,
And somehow the gold isn't all.

No! There's the land (Have you seen it?)
It's the cussedest land that I know,
From the big, dizzy mountains that screen it
To the deep, deathlike valleys below.
Some say God was tired when He made it;
Some say it's a fine land to shun.
Maybe, but there's some as would trade it
For no land on earth--and I'm one.

You come to get rich (damned good reason).
You feel like an exile at first.
You hate it like hell for a season,
And then you are worse than the worst.
It grips you like some kinds of sinning.
It twists you from foe to a friend.
It seems it's been since the beginning.
It seems like it will be to the end.

I've stood on some mighty mouthed hollow
That's plumb full of hush to the brim.
I've watched the big, husky sun wallow

In crimson and gold, and grow dim,
Till the moon set the pearly peaks gleaming,
And the stars tumbled out, neck and crop.
And I've thought that I surely was dreaming,
With the peace of the world piled on top.

The summer—no sweeter was ever.
The sunshiny woods all athrill.
The grayling aleap in the river.
The bighorn asleep on the hill.
The strong life that never knows harness.
The wilds where the caribou call.
The freshness, the freedom, the farness—
O God, how I'm stuck on it all!

The winter! the brightness that blinds you,
The white land locked tight as a drum,
The cold fear that follows and finds you
The silence that bludgeons you dumb.
The snows that are older than history,
The woods where the weird shadows slant:
The stillness, the moonlight, the mystery,
I've bade them good-bye—but I can't.

There's a land where the mountains are nameless,
And the rivers all run God knows where.
There are lives that are erring and aimless,
And deaths that just hang by a hair.
There are hardships that nobody reckons.
There are valleys unpeopled and still.
There's a land—oh, it beckons and beckons,
And I want to go back--and I will.

They're making my money dimmish.
I'm sick of the taste of champagne.
Thank God! When I'm skinned to a finish
I'll pike to the Yukon again.
I'll fight –and you bet it's no sham-fight.
It's hell! but I've been there before.
And it's better than this by a damn sight—
So me for the Yukon once more.

There's gold, and it's haunting and haunting.
It's luring me on as of old.
Yet it isn't the gold that I'm wanting
So much as just finding the gold.
It's the great, big, broad land 'way up yonder,
It's the forests where silence has lease,
It's the beauty that thrills me with wonder,
It's the stillness that fills me with peace.

CHAPTER ONE

I n his twenties, Justin Shaw, known as "Shorty," was five feet four, soft-spoken and unassuming—not the traits associated with the titan of industry he would later become. Deep-set eyes projected an intense look that made his classmates shy away. Serious when it comes to his studies, he welcomed the isolation. The Shaw family being well-to-do, Shorty's life had been planned out for him—private school followed by seven years at Harvard followed by an advanced degree in business from the University of Chicago. After all of that, he was expected to join his father's Boston law firm.

While in school, Shorty wrestled with one formidable restriction imposed by his father, Archer Shaw—no alcohol— a directive that turned out badly. On the day before he was leaving for college, his father called him into the library at home to give him some parting instructions.

"If you think I'm not serious about the alcohol question, think again. I will not invite a drunk into my law firm. On top of that, you will forfeit your inheritance."

The tone of his voice indicated to Shorty that his father meant what he said.

A serious student, Shorty had no time for frivolity or womanizing during his school years. Though quiet and reserved, no one who had spent time with him would have described him as boring. Shorty wasn't overly handsome, but attractive enough to interest any woman keen on men of high intelligence and good breeding. Occasional somber moods made him appear mysterious. Straight black hair and thick black brows enhanced the mystique, but a quick smile that was readily forthcoming affirmed his underlying affability.

Shorty graduated from business school and felt a craving for alcohol from years of abstinence. Out of curiosity he took one drink at a graduation party—and never stopped. Unfortunately, a month after the final graduation party, his mother and father were killed in a carriage accident. Soon after, he moved west to live with an uncle in San Francisco only to discover that the uncle had died of consumption a few days before his arrival. That put him in a dilemma workwise. He couldn't seek a legal job because he hadn't passed the California bar. Worse still, he had only a small amount of money to tide him over before finding suitable work. By then, the Boston lawyers back home had gobbled up every penny in his parents' estate by charging outlandish fees and absconding with the rest. With only a few dollars left, Shorty rented a room in a boardinghouse in downtown San Francisco where he planned to take time to consider his options.

The owner of the boardinghouse introduced herself as Libby Winters and a friendship between them quickly developed. Soon he became her assistant cook, handyman and chief helper. Libby always referred to him as Justin, and he soon fell in love with the copper-colored hair, and blue-eyed woman. She had a way of holding her head, placing her hands, crossing her legs that assured any onlooker, especially Shorty, that she was a woman of class, despite her position as owner of a cheap boardinghouse. There was never a harsh word from her, never any displays of temper. Her soft, melodious voice was a rich elixir, and he soon lost any desire to leave. Disarmed by her beauty, Shorty would fumble for words in her presence, often forgetting what he had intended to say. Her mere smile aroused a whirlwind of emotion. Best of all, in her mid-twenties, she wasn't that much older than he, although she was a few inches taller. Shy in her presence, he said nothing about his true feelings.

The work in the boardinghouse was non-stop, particularly when all ten rooms were filled. There were clothes and sheets to wash, meals to prepare, and rooms to clean, repairs to be made and cooking chores to be done. Soon the favorable reputation of the boardinghouse began to attract boarders. The location close to the docks enticed crane handlers, stevedores, ship crews and roustabouts. All ten boarders would gather in the hallway each night awaiting dinner, creating an all-to-familiar scene:

"Miss Libby, you're feeding us too well. Look at this belly."

"Josh, you had that belly when you came here," she said.

"I don't think it was this big, though," he said, as he rubbed it slowly.

"What's for dinner?" asked another patron.

"Ben, you'll just have to wait and see," she said.

From the hallway they could see Justin emerge out of the kitchen carrying two large platters of meatloaf.

"Come and get it, boys," he said. "It's Libby's famous recipe."

Most of the men wore work clothes—bib overalls, work pants, suspenders, black work shoes, vests over work shirts, sleeves rolled to the elbow. Libby permitted such dress during meals so long as faces and hands were clean. The absence of chit-chat and the rattling of silverware provided evidence of how well her meatloaf and other staples were received. The breadbaskets were filled several times, and seconds were routinely had by all. Shorty would refill the baskets and pour the water.

"Miss Libby, what's for dessert?" One of the boarders asked.

"Apple cobbler. It's your favorite, Clem," she said.

After dessert, the boarders would return to their rooms. Each of the men were nice enough, but none made Libby's heart sing. New arrivals would often make passes at her but backed off quickly when they realized she had no interest.

"I love them all, but I'm not in love with any of them," she would tell Shorty.

No surprise there. The boarders were a scruffy bunch. *But why doesn't she have romantic interest in me? Why am I a friend and nothing more? If that won't change, why do I stay?* Shorty wondered about that often until he realized that he had stayed only because he was deeply in love with her.

Libby found herself alone and childless after her hapless husband died suddenly of a massive heart attack five years before. She reverted to her maiden name, Winters, not as a rebuke but as part of her search for identity. Thankfully, before his death her husband purchased the boardinghouse and made her the sole owner. Running a boardinghouse was professionally unrewarding and only moderately lucrative. Libby wanted more and often longed to run off to find wealth and adventure.

Libby needed a partner to help her run the place and handle many of its mundane tasks. In the second year after Shorty's arrival, she offered him a partnership, which he gladly accepted. By then, she had become aware that her dearest friend was a closet drinker. It was a simple matter of counting the empty whisky bottles he deposited in the trash each week. She had no objection to his drinking so long as he remained sober and sharp during the day.

Just like Libby, Shorty had grown tired and bored with his position. *This is not why I came out West,* he would often think. No riches were to be had busing tables and serving water in a boardinghouse. So, when news arrived in 1896 of a massive gold strike in the Klondike, Shorty became ecstatic. Not only would it be his ticket out of Dullsville, but it might also give him an opportunity to win Libby's love by striking it rich. Others had similar notions. Within the space of a week, all ten of Libby's boarders headed north to prospect for gold.

"Lib, let's follow them, unless you have reservations about getting rich," Shorty proposed.

"I can't sell this boardinghouse fast enough to suit me," she said.

Before leaving San Francisco, Shorty studied pertinent material in the local library, particularly any available maps. When the boardinghouse sale was complete, the duo booked passage on the *Excelsior*, a steamer out of San Francisco headed for Skagway, a one-horse town in the Alaska Territory. Out of Skagway they would take White Pass, an overland trail known to provide access to the Yukon River, a treacherous waterway that would carry them downriver to Dawson City in the Yukon Territory of Canada. Dawson was located at the confluence of the Yukon and Klondike Rivers.

As their journey progressed, Shorty grew hopeful that Libby would fall in love with him, at last. With the money from mining, they could buy a nice house in San Francisco and live happily ever after, and in time, he could surely put his educational background into play in a way that would bring her even more riches and social status.

"Lib, once we get to Bennett Lake, we'll have to build a boat to carry us downriver to Dawson. You should know that there are treacherous river conditions on the Yukon River."

"You mean *white water rapids?*"

"That's what they say."

"I'm game if you are."

"Damn straight I am."

On board the *Excelsior*, Shorty was approached by a stranger named Jefferson Smith who had noticed Libby and asked to be introduced to her. He boarded the steamer at one of its brief stops in Alaska. Smith's gambling pursuits onboard did not prevent him from coming on deck from time to time to talk with Libby. Justin could only stand meekly by, fuming over the slick-talking, handsome man with a coal-black beard who favored neatly pressed tweed suits. Shortly could tell immediately that Smith was a sharpie, perhaps even a con artist and certainly a heavy gambler, and charmer. By the end of the voyage, Smith was referring to Libby as "Irish Eyes." Libby, smitten, felt love for the first time in years.

Smith announced his intentions to stay in Skagway permanently, whereas Skagway for Shorty and Libby was merely a stop on the way to the goldfields. Temporary or not, Shorty remained guarded, staying close to Libby whenever Smith appeared. Much to his dismay, shortly before the arrival in Skagway Libby announced that her plans had changed; she was going to remain in Skagway to operate a boardinghouse that she intended to purchase with Smith. Rooms for rent were in short supply in Skagway, Smith explained, and Libby could charge goldminers and travelers exorbitant fees that would make her rich.

Shorty prided himself on not showing his emotions. He was crushed by the change in plans but said little to dissuade Libby. After all, she had never pretended to be in love with him, and by her flushed face and downward stare, he could tell that she was vexed about disappointing her trusted friend. That provided Shorty some solace, but the news cut him deeply and when she enlightened him, he turned abruptly and walked to the far end of the deck.

That man is a scoundrel, Shorty thought, his lawyer instincts on full alert.

Shorty was not far wrong. Jefferson "Soapy" Smith had chosen Skagway as his base of operations because it provided one of the few access points to the gold-rich Klondike. The town had emerged as a nexus for stampeders and scores of well heeled travelers looking for adventure and opportunity further north. Smith's plan was to assemble a gang of hoodlums to fleece the vulnerable travelers and naïve prospectors and use his ill-gotten gains to amass wealth and power. It was a scheme he was well practiced at. In Colorado he had set up a similar operation.

Shorty recognized early on that Smith was his nemesis. The mere presence of the blackguard put his plans into disarray. As a result, Shorty was forced to brave the wilderness without his first love. He knew he would be thinking of Libby all the time he was there. Upon his return, he was convinced that he would win her with his riches. Angry and frustrated, he left her on the dock the day they arrived in Skagway and never looked back. His only solace, he knew, would come from alcohol and he was anxious to get started.

As he searched for the nearest saloon, Shorty fumed. *But for the gold rush this piss-hole of a town wouldn't even be on the map.* His description of Skagway was apt. The town in 1896 was an ugly place positioned over what was once a steaming swamp. In the heat of summer, odoriferous emissions stung the nostrils of anyone foolish enough to remain outside for any extended period. The town wasn't much to look at even without the stink. It began as a conglomeration of log shacks and tents, which offered few amenities, and over time its layout hadn't changed much. The main street, known as Broadway, remained nothing more than deep ruts cut into black mud. Though the mud made it difficult to cross the street during dry times, it was much worse when the rain turned the street into a treacherous soup that could easily swallow a small dog. Except for business generated by the saloons, Clancy's being the most popular, commerce was negligible. It did have one advantage, however. Being on the water, Skagway was the sole point of entry for anyone intending to tackle White Pass, the main trail out of Skagway leading to the Klondike. At the height of the gold rush, so many vessels arrived in Skagway's harbor with cargo and passengers that Skagway's main beach was continually overrun.

CHAPTER TWO

Purely by accident Shorty ran into Rudy Jenkins, a brilliant scholar who had been a year ahead of him in law school. Rudy had tried private practice with a large Seattle firm only to discover after a few years that he hated what he was doing. A switch to an in-house counsel position was equally unrewarding. Then came word of the gold rush and Rudy, like Shorty, jumped in with both feet. Neither Shorty nor Rudy knew that the other was in town the evening of Shorty's arrival in Skagway. Shorty spotted Rudy sitting at the bar in Clancy's.

"Hey, Harvard boy, are you glued to that seat?"

Rudy turned on his stool.

"My God, it's Shorty Shaw."

They exchanged hugs.

"What are you doing here? Rudy asked.

"Same as you."

"Yeah, let's get some gold," Rudy laughed.

"Hey, maybe we can prospect together. My proposed partner crumped out on me," Shorty said.

"You can bet on it. I'm looking for a partner myself."

They moved to an empty booth, one of Clancy's ratty versions that is most often unoccupied at that time of day. By the end of an hour, they'd discussed personal history on both sides, the whereabouts of old school chums, the desire to get rich, a review of what equipment they'd need for their adventure and, finally, a pledge by both to work together. Inevitably, Libby's name came up.

"She and I were set to go to the diggings together. We planned to work side by side. Once into it, I planned to ask her to marry me."

"You mean, after you got rich?"

"Yeah, that's correct, *if* we got rich."

"Where is she now?"

"The Skagway hotel," Shorty said.

"That place is a dump. You need to get her out of there. Come stay with me. I've got a decent-enough place and she can stay there after we leave."

"We accept," Shorty laughed, then grimaced.

Rudy quickly got the gist of what was happening. Shorty was hurting and his pain was easy to detect—clenched fists, a cracking voice, grinding teeth

"She stole my heart," Shorty confessed, chasing his words with a shot of whisky.

"I can see that. Did you ever tell her about your feelings?"

"Hell no. I can't stand rejection," Shorty said.

"You're friends and nothing more?"

"To her we are. But I'd hoped to change things during our stay in the gold fields. It was a perfect setup. She was as excited about going as I was. Then this bastard comes along to ruin everything by bribing her with the promise of a boardinghouse if she stayed in Skagway. He's a slick talker and just as slimy as the snake that stuck it to Eve in the Garden of Eden. He sweet-talked her sure as hell."

"You haven't told me this fellow's name."

"Jefferson Smith."

"Oh, my stars. If it's the guy I am thinking of, his nickname is *Soapy*. He was notorious in Seattle, and in Denver before that. He has a group of thieves who follow him around like trained dogs. In short order, he controls a town by spreading bribe money around. At best he's a grifter, at worst he's a murderer. Tell Libby to get rid of him."

"Too late. I think she's fallen for him."

"Maybe she'll eventually see through him," Rudy offered.

"I wish there was something I could do to protect her from him."

"For now, why don't you offer to let her stay at my place in town."

"That would be great," Shorty said.

"Our connection is Godsent, I swear," Rudy said. "With both of us looking for partners and all."

Shorty left his friend and found Libby in the lobby of the hotel, awaiting a room. Even in his bruised state, Shorty offered assistance. He told her about Rudy's wood-framed rental unit.

Libby was delighted to make the change.

"It'll just be sitting vacant while we're prospecting."

"That's so kind of you and Rudy," Libby said, softly kissing Shorty on the cheek. "That'll tide me over until Jefferson and I get our boardinghouse open."

Shorty's heart sunk further.

Shorty and Ruby began the next day planning their trip. Both agreed that White Pass out of Skagway was the best bet, even though day or night the trail would be jammed with stampeders intent on making a killing in the gold fields and unwilling to give ground to anything standing in their way.

"Greed is always the common denominator with these sub-humans," Rudy said.

The rush had begun several months earlier when news of the strike trickled into the states. Shorty and Rudy were late, they knew, but both also knew that the rule of first come, first served was still in place, assuming they could find a spot that hadn't been staked out already. Rudy and Shorty figured it would take at least a week to pull together the necessary gear.

While at Clancy's, Rudy and Shorty had made a list of the items they would need: back packs, hiking boots, fire starter kits, extra sets of footwear and clothing, numerous pairs of underwear and socks, a pup tent for each of them, canned goods, salted beef, and as many jugs of water as they can fit on their carry-sled, and that was only the beginning. They were now ready and optimistic.

CHAPTER THREE

After a disappointing year, Shorty returned to Skagway without his friend and partner and without a significant amount of gold. Rudy had died of consumption during the winter. After his return. Shorty became a regular at Clancy's on Saturdays with his drinking crew—Doc, Wolfy, Artez and Tenderfoot. They would come early to get their special booth close to the back door, a location necessitated by the risk of shootouts, which were common in Clancy's on Saturdays, the day on which every man in town—townies, miners, and greenhorns alike—showed up at Clancy's to get drunk and socialize. The saloon was a log structure built with little attention to amenities such as wall covering or indoor plumbing, the latter omission being confirmed by the oversized outhouse out back, and the long line of patrons always waiting to use it despite the overpowering stench.

By noon on one Saturday, the din of noise and conversation became overpowering, and the presence of cigar and cigarette smoke made it difficult to see. Most of the customers, beer mugs in hand, stood shoulder to shoulder unable to move, let alone find empty tables or booths. The crowd was a seedy bunch. Shorty and Tenderfoot were the only two in the room lacking facial hair. Tenderfoot had arrived too recently to be taken in by the temptation to grow a beard, and Shorty figured he might as well remain clean shaven since he would soon be bald. By contrast, Wolfy and Artez both had full beards, thick and dark, hitting at mid-chest, and Doc sported a neat grey handlebar. As with most full beards in the room, those favored by Wolfy and Artez were littered with spittle and food chunks. Four of the five at Shorty's table wore unwashed breeches, Klondike shirts made of heavy wool, braces, and high leather boots with rawhide laces. They also wore wool caps, rarely removed. Doc was the exception. He was bareheaded lest a hat or cap interfere with his magnificent mane of white hair. His buckskin shirt and pants were spotless.

"Tenderfoot, you look as jerky as the tip of a cow's tail," said Wolfy.

"I'm agitated is all . . . damn you all! You did it. Why the hell can't I?" Tenderfoot asked.

"Artez and me, we wuz lucky. Ain't no two ways 'bout that. We wuz already here when word of the strike got out. The timing makes all the difference, it be played out or staked out by now," Wolfy said.

"Even if the gold were there in unstaked areas, which it ain't," Artez added, "getting to the goldfields is no easy chore. White Pass into the Canadian Yukon is murder. And that's just to Bennett Lake. From there you've got to survive the rapids on the Yukon River."

"Only a few made it all the way, and fewer still found any gold after they arrived. Like I said many times, the gold is either staked out or played out," Wolfy said.

Shorty found it tough to guess the age of the two ex-miners—they could in their forties or even fifties—but he also knew that Doc at age sixty was comfortable with his elder status, though the white hair and mustache made it impossible for him to take any other position.

Artez tried again.

"Many a stampeder lost his life or property or both along the trail to into Dawson City or fighting the rapids on the Yukon River. Those with any sense turn and run from them rapids like a scalded dog. Now that the gold is gone, there's no reason to take the risk. If you think otherwise, you're mistook.

"The rapids will probably do you in," Wolfy added. "On top of that, you'll have to face thieves along the way who will be lying in wait at every turn. Success is a long shot."

Wolfy lowered his voice and leaned in close to whisper as he hinted at thievery along the trail. He knew full well that many of the robberies are planned by Soapy Smith. Considering the din, however, he need not have worried about being overheard by any of Soapy's allies.

Shorty explained that his experience had been quite different than that of Artez and Wolfy because the two miners arrived early whereas he and Rudy arrived late. He and his partner had no luck even though they were only a few months past the initial strike. They had uncovered little to no gold in unstaked areas even after months of back-killing work.

"We were delayed," Shorty said. "Rudy and I had a bad experience on White Pass."

"What happened?" Doc asked.

"We used a carry-sled for our goods, but most of the rabble purchased pack horses or mules in Skagway. Overloaded and starving, these animals were abused so badly that Rudy and I could witness it no longer. We turned back and took the Chilkoot Pass out of Dyea. With the doubling back we lost several days."

"Why did you turn back?" asked Doc.

"The trail was jammed belly to belly. Those who had horses or mules to carry packs treated them so badly that Rudy and I began to get spooked. The poor animals were screaming in pain most of the time. Their backs turned bloody under the excessive loads. If they broke a leg or got stuck in a bog, the greed-stricken rabble would pass right over them."

"What happened to Rudy?" Tenderfoot asked.

"Died at the diggings of consumption," Shorty said, sipping his beer.

"There is one location in the trail known as Dead Horse Pass. The name is appropriate because the ravine below it is where the bastards throw their discarded animals. There are carcasses down below, hundreds of them. Horses and mules are shot and then pushed over the side. Often, they're pushed without being shot to save ammunition."

Tenderfoot listened intently as Shorty continued.

"It is worse than you can imagine. Judging from the human-like screams from below, it becomes obvious that some of the poor animals are still alive when they hit bottom. No one seemed to care. One man beat a horse on the trail so severely that it dropped in place and expired. The rabble passed over the carcass without stopping. One poem I found later captures the gist of it."

"A poem?" Tenderfoot asked.

"Yes. I copied it from one of the newspapers in Dawson. Don't know who wrote it. The title is 'Do Horses Think of Suicide?' I've my copy here in my backpack. Let me read it to you:

> Dead Horse Pass was the spot
> during the Klondike Gold Rush
> where many a packhorse was shot,
> and then pushed into the ravine below.
> The story goes that one brave mare,
> bloody and abused, charged over the edge
> with valuable packs in place
> before any firearm could be used.
> Was it an equine suicide?
> Many of us felt it so,
> a sacrifice by a poor animal,
> terrified and confused,
> aware of a man with a rifle up ahead
> and rocked by the screaming
> coming from the horses down below.
> That the mare could make such a heroic stand
> was welcome news for a few of us
> who saw it as a final equine rebellion
> both courageous and grand."

"I give that poet high marks," Doc said.

Shorty nodded.

"One scene I'll never forget," he said. "Two oxen refused to go any farther, even when the man leading them began beating them with a metal rod. They were completely played out. At that point, the sadistic bastard set a fire underneath them. Still, they couldn't move, so he roasted them both alive."

"Good Lord," Tenderfoot said.

"By then we're as anxious as a pregnant fox in a forest fire to get out of there. A rational human being can witness such brutality only so long. The fate of those two oxen was the tipping point. We turned back . . . and gladly," Shorty said.

"Yeah, you turn back, but the only other trail available is the Chilkoot out of Dyea, which presents similar difficulties, I'm sure," Tenderfoot said.

"Anything is better than what we observed on White Pass. Greed was turning those gold seekers into animals. Fortunately, fewer pack animals were necessary out of Dyea because the Chilkoot Trail was relatively level, at least in the beginning. But the turnaround time caused us a significant delay," Shorty said.

"I refuse to believe that all the gold is gone," Tenderfoot said.

"Let me put it this way. All the good diggings are staked out, and what's left is not worth much. We found that out the hard way," Shorty said.

"And if you wait too long, you'll have to deal with ravaging weather," Doc said. "Why, I heard of a miner who froze to death last year while tying his shoelaces. Happened as he was bending over. They had to bury him in a bass drum."

"Very funny," Tenderfoot said after the laughing subsided.

From the glint in Tenderfoot's eye, Shorty could see that further arguments would be useless. Shorty had seen it before. Once people made up their minds to go north, most often there was no stopping them. Shorty was aware of this phenomenon because he experienced it himself.

Wolfy interrupted.

"Even if you do decide to go, you can't leave now. You wouldn't make it to Dawson before the freeze."

"You mean I'm stuck in this godforsaken town 'til spring?" Tenderfoot asked

"Looks that way—less you can fly like a bird," Wolfy said laughing.

Tenderfoot shook his head. "I'm fucked," he said, convinced at last that he had lost the debate.

"Hush yer mouthing," Artez said. "There's no need to get hystericky. We just tryin' ta help."

While sipping on his beer, Shorty thought back on his Klondike experience. Just getting to Dawson City was hell on earth. The back-breaking trek over the Chilkoot trail to Lake Lindemann at the headwaters of the Yukon River was grueling. Rudy and Shorty had to use a rip saw to transform logs into planks for use in a crude rivercraft. Neither Shorty or Rudy had ever used a rip saw, and neither ended the procedure with good feelings about ever doing it again. When the craft was ready for launching, neither man had a sense of accomplishment, only continuing pain, particularly when the boat threatened to capsize more than once during the downriver ride.

When they finally spotted Dawson from afar, the tiny town looked like an enchanted city. The Ogilvie Mountain Range to the north added a scenic touch, and in the fading light of evening the peaks took on a purple cast. As their craft got closer the enchantment had become overridden by drabness attributable to log and frame structures set in neat rows with only one hotel, the Occidental, in evidence.

Shorty recalled the initial entry into Dawson when he and Rudy first discovered that the rumors about the town's ugliness were not exaggerated. It was a dirt-water town of the first order that becomes a hub in the gold fields only because of its central location. The early arrivals had discovered two creeks known as Rabbit and Little Rabbit, which became Bonanza and Eldorado, respectively, a name change for both when gold was discovered along their banks. Unfortunately, Rudy and Shortly had missed that gravy train.

Despite the treachery and danger of prospecting, the two men had learned that a single pan of paydirt could produce as much as one thousand dollars in gold, or more. But no such luck was bestowed upon them. Their panning yielded only dirt, forcing them to give it up in favor of digging operations into hard ground, which uncovered only deep muck. The subsequent sluicing operations that began in the spring when water began to flow freely were equally unrewarding.

One piece of luck did come when they discovered an abandoned cabin a few miles upriver. Their enthusiasm waned, however, when they discovered that the cabin was vermin infested with no protection from mosquitoes, gnats, and sand flies that tormented them constantly. Worst of all, when temperatures plummeted, the wind whistled through cracks in the walls as if the walls were not there at all. In such weather conditions, their sheet-iron stove had to operate continuously and the task of finding or buying firewood became a constant nightmare.

Their only respite came on the rare occasions when Shorty and Rudy pulled themselves loose from digging operations and headed for town. Shorty and Rudy assumed that Dawson would be wide open and lawless, but they were surprised to find that, unlike Skagway, it was a relatively peaceful because of the iron grip applied by the Canadian Mounties. Sidearms, for example, were forbidden in the city. Soon the two new arrivals discovered that whatever restrictions applied to the town in general did not apply at all to the red-light district along Front Street, where the pulse of the city could be found. In three or four blocks, brothels, parlor houses, and cribs were crowded together with saloons, dance halls and gaming houses.

Continuing to sip his beer and ruminate, Shorty chaffed at the smell caused principally by Dawson's way of handling raw sewage, which ran along trenches at the side of the various roads. How he and Rudy had escaped the ravages of typhoid fever, he would never know. One thing was certain, however. Neither man would risk another type of disease that was likely to come from foolish forays in the part of town inhabited by the "soiled doves" that inhabited the structures and tents along Front Street. A social disease wasn't welcomed by miners who had been subjected to adversity in all its raw forms for weeks and months on end in the goldfields. But a few sex-starved onlookers always took the bait.

Shorty recalled how he and Rudy would find chairs close to the Faro table to watch as large fortunes were won or lost. They would take a similar passive approach in the dance halls where they watched from afar as the rich patrons filled the private boxes, bringing with them two or three soubrettes. To Shorty, it had seemed like the dandies in their dark suits and bowler hats were hell-bent to spend or give away as much of their fortunes as possible. They were the ones who had come to the gold fields early and struck it rich, quickly making them anxious to spend without restraint. Other sourdoughs arrived without concern for restrictions upon their dress, wearing dirty trousers, soiled shirts, muddy boots, and lopsided fur hats while carrying totes full of gold. If a dancehall girl was particularly enchanting while performing on the tiny stages afforded to them, they were rewarded with an avalanche of nuggets thrown by responsive and well-heeled onlookers.

On one night, out of curiosity, Shorty followed one of these high-fliers to see how many dance halls he would inhabit before becoming too drunk to stand. The man swung through the Monte Carlo, the Combination, the Palace Grand and two saloons. At the end of his travels his tote was empty, and any hint of sobriety long gone. Shorty would never forget the sounds of the city that greeted them when they first arrived, raucous laughter, barking dogs, high-pitched screams, loud conversations, and the constant belting of barker's voices enhanced by megaphones touting the enticements found inside the gaming houses and dance halls. Such establishments had offered their own cacophony in the form of rattling pianos playing ragtime. Shorty and Rudy had been shocked to find that all boisterous activity went silent on Sundays when the Blue Laws were in effect. For that single day, all business in the city shut down, or else.

Shorty ruminated over his last days with Rudy, who was struck with consumption caused by frigid temperatures and bad food at their frigid, small cabin. Even though Shorty escaped pneumonia's ugly reach, Rudy did not. Shorty felt a tug on his heart as he remembered Rudy's tortured face looking up at him from his deathbed. He cared for his partner as best he could, but there was no way to stop the ravages of the disease without a doctor on hand to help. Rudy's casket was lodged in a shed in town until the spring thaw made the ground accessible.

Doc studied Shorty for a minute, noting his friend's somberness and solitude, even amid the boisterousness around him.

"Looks like Shorty's pretty down," Doc whispered to Wolfy.

"Yeah, he looks kinda glum."

Doc held his nose "What the hell you been eating, Wolfy? Your breath could curdle milk or strip a pine tree bare."

"It's that partner of mine, Doc. He's got me eatin' garlic twenty-four hours a day. He figgers it'll prolong my life."

"It's the truth, Doc. I read it somewheres," Artez answered.

"Well, if you keep at it, you'll damn sure discover what solitude is like, I can tell you that."

Even Shorty grinned.

"I've got two questions for you," Tenderfoot said to Shorty.

"Fire away," Shorty said.

"Who the hell was Soapy Smith, and how did he come to be killed?"

Shorty smiled to himself. *It never fails.* Whenever newcomers arrived in Skagway, any conversation at Clancy's eventually got around to Soapy Smith, the former owner.

"Jefferson Randolph 'Soapy' Smith was Skagway's most notorious criminal before he got himself killed in a shootout," Shorty said.

"Tell me more," Tenderfoot pleaded.

Shortly after Shorty and Rudy had left Skagway to seek their fortunes, Smith had purchased the boardinghouse for Libby. He already owned two saloons, Clancy's, and a smaller bar across the street called Jeff Smith's Parlor. When he first arrived, Smith had placed the town marshal and other elected officials on his payroll, which allowed his gang of hoodlums to steal without the threat of reprisal. The town had become wide open and lawless, with Smith acting behind the scenes. Shorty explained that at the time of Smith's death at the age of thirty-eight, the gang controlled most of the criminal activity, not only in Skagway, but also along the primary trails out of Skagway leading to the Klondike. Shorty didn't mention his first encounter with Smith on the *Excelsior*. He wanted to avoid making any reference to Libby.

Shorty pointed out to Tenderfoot that some of the characters who came to Skagway didn't come to dig, adding that Soapy was one of those. He and his gang were content to stay in the area because the pickings were good. Stampeders loaded with cash or gold were always at hand.

"The only reason Soapy didn't move on to Dawson is because the Mounties won't let him cross the border into Canada after learning of his misdeeds. They were aware that the law forced him out of Colorado," Shorty said.

Doc jumped into the conversation. "There are varying opinions about Soapy. To me, he was a friend."

Doc explained that when he lost his license to practice medicine because of excessive drinking, Soapy continued to use his services and encouraged others to do the same, thereby keeping his favorite physician out of the poorhouse. Doc added that Soapy was a candidate for greatness at birth who took the wrong path.

"He could have been whatever he wanted to be—statesman, lawyer, preacher, business tycoon, even a banker. Highly educated, he came from a well-to-do Georgia family. Three of his brothers became lawyers and three bankers. Soapy was brilliant, a great orator," Doc said.

"Trouble is he had a strong hankering to cheat people," Shorty interjected.

Doc pointed to a photograph of Soapy hanging on the wall behind the bar. Tenderfoot stood to make his way unsteadily in that direction. He returned a short time later.

"Soapy was a handsome man," Tenderfoot announced.

"Damn straight," Doc said.

Doc continued his favorable monologue, describing Soapy's desire to be the best at everything he did including his criminal endeavors.

"With the objective of mastering a ruse known as the shell game, Soapy went to a shell-game expert and asked for lessons, which made him one of the best in the business."

"How did he get his name?" Tenderfoot asked.

Shorty answered. "Soapy at one time sold cakes of soap by telling people that in some cases money was stuffed under the soap wrappers. With the help of a shill, he convinced the onlookers that a five-dollar bill was waiting for them to discover. Of course, his customers never found anything inside. One time the police arrested him and wrote down the name *Soapy* on the police blotter when they couldn't think of his real name. The handle stuck."

Doc then volunteered a long description of Soapy's operations that, to Shorty's annoyance, made him appear to be a modern-day Robin Hood.

"The man lived by a code. He never cheated a local or any woman. He even started a fund for the benefit of stray dogs."

"Sure, Doc, then he sold the dogs at a big profit to prospectors," Shorty said.

"Don't be so unkind. Many a widow in Skagway received money from him."

"Come on, Doc. Those were the same widows whose husbands were killed by members of his gang."

"Soapy was never convicted of any killing. In fact, he's never even been charged. If gang members got out of hand, he generally banished them, but he couldn't always control them."

"Tell Tenderfoot about the fake telegraph line and the phony assay office," Wolfy said.

At that point, Doc excused himself to go to the privy. With Doc away, Shorty became big-headed in the way he presented Soapy's scams. One favorite, he said, was the telegraph caper in which Soapy's operators charged five dollars per telegram even though there were no lines up into Skagway at the time. What's worse, according to Shorty he made sure the fake replies came *collect*. He also described the fake assay office where miners were stripped of stashes that had taken months to accumulate.

"Another scam was the recruiting caper involving innocent victims who thought they were signing up for service in the Spanish-American War. While a so-called doctor performed "physicals" inside a tent, someone else was going through their belongings. Another ploy was to plant a gang member on the arriving steamers whose job was to cozy up to prospective targets. The objective was to find out where the money was. Other gang members then would lead these suckers to the slaughter after they debarked. Most of the victims returned home voluntarily after being separated from their valuables. Soapy always gave them passage money."

"He could afford to do that. In his prime, Soapy was making big money," Wolfy said.

"Why didn't the victims go to the law?" Tenderfoot asked.

"The marshal was in cahoots. Soapy paid him well," Shorty said.

"What brought Soapy down," Tenderfoot asked.

At that point, Doc returned.

"I can handle that one, Shorty," Doc said.

Doc explained that an "unbalanced prospector" did him in.

"How did it happen?" Tenderfoot asked.

Doc gave details.

"And Soapy ends up dead?" Tenderfoot asked.

"Yes. And Frank Reid, the leader of the vigilante group, also died."

"Doc, did you attend Soapy's funeral?" Shorty asked.

"Yes."

"Who all was present?" Shorty asked.

"Just me, his gang, and one other person . . . a woman."

"Did you know her?" Shorty asked.

"No, but I do know it wasn't his wife."

"His wife!" Shorty exclaimed.

"Why, sure. Didn't you know? They separated in Colorado when she reached her limit regarding his gambling and drinking and carousing. Still, he never divorced her. In fact, he waited anxiously for her letters each week, which came regular as clockwork to cheer him up," Doc said.

"Now, that's a bit of news I wasn't aware of," Shorty said. "I never knew he was married. I swear I never did."

"Doc, how do you know that the woman at the funeral wasn't the wife?" Tenderfoot asked.

"Because I've seen that particular woman about town several times. She's quite the looker—red hair, blue eyes."

CHAPTER FOUR

On the day before the last day of his life, Soapy Smith had been sitting behind his desk at Jeff Smith's Parlor in Skagway, across the street from Clancy's. Some referred to this watering hole as City Hall since it was the well-known center of gang criminal activity in the area. Soapy was conferring with Van B. Triplett, one of the members of his gang. Tripp, known as "Old Man Tripp," was in his fifties. With gray hair, he had the look of a preacher or judge about him, a kindly look that a potential target would trust implicitly.

"How bad is it, Tripp?"

"Real bad, Boss. Our backs are to the wall. The boys fleeced the wrong sourdough this time."

"Who is it?"

"A stampeder nobody ever heard of by the name of J.D. Stewart, freshly arrived from the Klondike."

Rather than get his hands dirty panning for gold or shaking down a victim, Soapy remained in Skagway waiting word of the outcome of the operations he had helped to plan. Occasionally, one of the targets ended up dead. Even when the act was unintentional, the gang member responsible was inevitably sent packing, a risk that all gang members were aware of.

"How much did we get?" Soapy asked.

"A stash of gold worth twenty-eight hundred."

"Whoa. That kind of money is worth fightin' for. How did we get it?"

"The boys rolled him."

In most cases, the victim would surrender the stolen property and leave by the next boat, glad to get out alive. Soapy always provided passage money. By contrast, Stewart was a real firebrand who began screaming the moment he realized that he'd been robbed. After several months expended in the diggings, hard noses like Stewart were not about to submit docilely to thievery. Instead, Stewart complained to the city fathers after the local marshal refused assistance. Undaunted, Stewart went to Dyea, a nearby town to seek assistance there.

Slim Foster, who had been riding hard from Dyea, entered the room. He was covered with trail dust that placed a thin coating over his jeans, Mackinaw, hat, and boots. His beard, usually coal black was brown and speckled from a gritty covering some of which fell on the floor as he removed the red bandana from his neck. He was breathing hard from the rigors of the trip.

"Boss, the bottom's dropped out. Dyea's marshal is coming to Skagway to join up with the Committee of 101. They've set up a meeting at Sperry's Warehouse."

The Committee of 101 was made up of Skagway citizens in favor of cleaning up the town. Soapy referred to them as "the goddamned vigilantes."

"Have a drink, Slim, on the house—and don't worry. I've got a few aces up my sleeve," Soapy said.

He was sitting in his desk chair, thinking. The gang members were aware that when Soapy was in a reflective mood, as was now occurring, the best course was to get out of his way. Both Slim and Tripp took up positions at the bar while Soapy turned in the chair and began to stare out the window.

Abruptly he turned back.

"Listen, boys, nothing more's going to happen today. Come back bright and early armed to the teeth. Everyone should plan to be here."

Soapy arrived early. By the time Tripp got there, his boss had been alone at his desk for at least an hour.

"You aren't going to like what I'm going to tell you," Tripp said.

"Try me."

"The Committee of 101 has set a deadline for you to return the gold or its value in dollars. The time set is four o'clock this afternoon."

"Who do they think they're dealing with?" His red face reflected his fury. "They can't give orders to Jefferson Smith, by God."

Soapy stood, his anger fully apparent on his face. Reaching for his Model 1892 Winchester, he made a pronouncement. "The only thing they'll get from me is lead!"

By this time, several other gang members had arrived. Because of the cramped quarters, Soapy decided to change the venue to Clancy's across the street. The drinks, of course, were on the house. There was a great whoop of approval and a shuffling of boots on the wooden floor at the proclamation. Smith placed his loaded rifle on the bar and began drinking shots. By late afternoon, he was totally soused.

"Tripp, has the deadline passed?" Smith slurred.

"Some time back."

"Then, it's time to go."

Smith grabbed his rifle, and there was another whoop of approval as the ranks opened to let him through. With Soapy in the lead, the group headed down State Street and out onto Juneau Wharf. Soapy was quickly spotted by the opposition whereupon the current leader, Frank Reid, and a few others came forward to meet him. When Reid and Soapy were almost toe to toe, Soapy pointed the Winchester at Reid whereupon Reid grabbed the end of the barrel. A struggle ensued. Still holding the barrel with one hand, Reid managed to shoot twice. One round struck Soapy in the chest. During the melee, Soapy's rifle discharged, producing an ugly wound in Reid's groin. Soapy's last words came just as Reid grabbed the barrel of the Winchester.

"For God's sake, man, don't shoot."

CHAPTER FIVE

I n the year Shorty was away from Skagway, he had prospected at various sites along the Klondike River near Dawson. When he returned to Skagway after giving up his quest, he returned empty-handed for the most part, and in short order, rented a room at Libby's boardinghouse. Anxious to hear about his experiences, Libby was delighted to see him. His plan was to rest up before traveling back to San Francisco, and he was hopeful Libby would join him now that Soapy was dead.

"Libby, I'll be going back. Won't you come with me?"

"Can't, it's too soon after his death."

"Why do you insist on mourning a worthless criminal?"

"I fell in love with him before I became aware of all that."

"Well, now that you know, you're free to go."

"It's not that simple. By the way, I was sorry to hear that your partner died."

They were seated at the kitchen table of the boardinghouse.

"Rudy was a good man. I'll miss him. He had a tough time at the end," Shorty said.

"He was certainly kind to me when he provided temporary quarters."

"He was a fine man who had a brilliant career ahead of him. I'll miss him terribly."

"You've always had a big heart," she said.

"I was at Clancy's this morning," Shorty said.

"Your favorite spot."

"We tried to educate Tenderfoot about some of Soapy's nefarious ventures—like the fake telegraph."

"Anyone stupid enough to fall for that one deserves to be fleeced," Libby huffed.

"And the cakes of soap."

"What do they say? There's a sucker born every minute."

"And the so-called recruiting caper."

"Oh, the dreams of young men."

"And the assay office that wasn't really an assay office—and the robberies—and the murders."

"Soapy himself never murdered anyone."

"And then there's this other thing."

"What other thing?"

"Soapy was married when he left Colorado, and he remained married."

"WHY THAT LOW-DOWN ROTTEN SON-OF-A-BITCH!"

Shorty was startled, having never heard Libby raise her voice in anger, let alone use profanity. *Libby might come with me after all,* Shorty thought. His hunch was right.

It didn't take Libby long to sell the boardinghouse, and the two boarded the *Excelsior* one week after the sale.

Looking at the water below, Libby stood at the rail of the *Excelsior* thinking.

He was married and never told me. How could he have been so deceitful? Did he really intend to marry me?

She turned to Shorty

"Justin, there's something I've got to tell you. I'm pregnant with Jefferson's child," she said, her face flushed and eyes fiery.

"Oh, my sweet Jesus. No wonder you were so upset."

Her auburn hair, usually done up neatly, was tied up in a casual knot atop her head. Even in such a disheveled state she projected a beauty that overwhelmed Shorty.

"He promised to marry me when I told him about it. He seemed pleased with the news. The one blessing is that no one in Skagway will ever know about the baby."

"I knew about it. One afternoon I followed your buggy to that small hotel outside of town. Soapy's white horse was tied up in front. It wasn't hard to figure out what the scenario was."

"Horrors," she said as she put both hands over her mouth.

"Libby, do you have any idea how that discovery tortured me? I fell in love with you the moment I first saw you, I—"

"Oh, Justin, don't say any more, please don't. Although you are my best friend, I have never felt that way about you."

Forlorn, Shorty escorted Libby back to California. They stayed in separate suites on the ship, spending very little time together. Even during meals, they were mostly silent. But on the trip, Libby started thinking practically about her plight. With a baby on the way, she would need financial security and the child would certainly benefit from having a father.

"Justin, I'll marry you on one condition," she said.

"Only one?"

"You must promise me that you'll give up drinking."

"What are you talking about?"

"Back when we worked together in the boardinghouse in San Francisco, I was able to count the bottles you consumed on a weekly basis by counting the empties hidden in the trash. I didn't complain because your job performance was never affected."

"You actually counted the bottles?"

"Yes, I did."

"Libby, I—"

"Do you promise?"

"Yes."

Two weeks after arriving in San Francisco, Libby and Justin were married. Good to his word, Shorty, stopped drinking, finding that the resulting clarity in thinking added to his confidence and ambition. The ceremony occurred before a justice of the peace in City Hall. Although her family didn't attend, Libby's brother sent money, enough when combined with the sale proceeds from the boardinghouse to pay for a similar facility in the city.

Libby and Shorty would often sit on the porch in the evenings, a favorite time of day when the street vendors appeared to offer an assortment of foods from their portable grills that never failed to arouse hunger: walnuts, various types of fish, chili, hamburger, cheese steak and other aromas that the two could savor from the porch.

"You've never told me much about your family," he said.

"I didn't think you were interested."

"Of course, I'm interested."

She told him that her father, Jason Winters, was a banker and did very well at his job until alcohol brought him down. He was fired for drinking while at work and soon the family couldn't afford to keep up their fine residence on the Main Line in Philadelphia. Anxious to turn his life around, her father was struck by the idea of going west, taking the family to Casper, Wyoming where he became an unsuccessful real estate agent, mainly because of his insobriety.

Libby described her mother, Alice, as ramrod tough, a woman who rarely showed her feelings, striking in appearance with auburn hair like Libby's, a woman kind and gentle despite her imposing demeanor. Libby also had a sister, Rebecca, whom she hadn't seen in years. Both Libby and Becky had attended the best private schools in Philadelphia and Casper, thanks to Alice's parents, who had money and paid for their granddaughters' schooling.

Bored with Casper, and longing again to be in a big city, Libby married Leonard Wilson, an aspiring lawyer who wanted to build a litigation practice in San Francisco. His practice was modest and to add income for the family he bought a boardinghouse for him and his bride, with financial help from Libby's mother.

After just a couple years of marriage, Wilson grew ill with cancer. Knowing his days were numbered, he deeded the boardinghouse to Libby. Her mother, Alice, died a year later, and Libby's father, died one month after that. Libby felt trapped again, never imagining her fate in life would be running a boardinghouse for grubby men.

Back in San Francisco, Libby and Shorty would often sit on the porch discussing their past, dreams, and fears.

"Won't this part of the city become a tinderbox if fire ever breaks out? she asked. "The houses are all so close together."

"Definitely. All structures here are wooden. That's why we've got to move."

Despite their reservations, all went well for several years. Shorty soon discovered his special talent as a businessperson. In short order, he was running companies tied to real estate, meat packing and shipping. He credited his success to his extensive education, but Libby was always quick to note that his decision to give up drinking cleared his head in a way that made him ready to face new challenges.

Vast amounts of money began to flow into their accounts. Soon they moved into a Victorian structure on Nob Hill built to Libby's specifications. The original structure was razed and replaced with a magnificent home. By then, Libby was living the life she had always envisioned for herself and found herself completely in love with Justin. As a lover, he far outranked Soapy to the point where she could no longer remember what sex with Soapy was like. With Justin, she emerged as a sexual being, something that never occurred with Soapy.

After one love session she laughed to herself thinking that the name "Shorty" was totally inappropriate for her well-endowed husband.

Gardening became a full-time pursuit for Libby, and Shorty was working ten-hour days and loving it. One glorious year followed another. Young Seth was healthy and happy. As the years sped by, Libby became even more beautiful, at least Shorty thought so. She was content to devote herself to him, handling the family finances. Even so, she began to worry that she was losing her identity. So, she accepted the presidency of the San Francisco Art Association. Volunteer work gave her a sense of purpose, but it did not quell her adventurous desires.

One morning they were relaxing on the veranda of their new home. Below, a portion of the city was bathed in light as the morning sun brought the pastel-colored structures to life, one at a time. The colors in Libby's potted geraniums and chrysanthemums on the front steps abruptly burst into flame as the sunlight reached them. Libby watched the scene unfold and wondered why she remained unsettled in the face of such splendor. She fell prey to a small voice in her head that kept telling her that the good times would soon end, giving her a feeling of impending doom.

"Justin, what could it be?" she had asked her husband. "Is it a premonition of bad consequences. I've never had such a feeling before."

She wondered whether her negative attitude might be a product of her guilt for being unappreciative of the good life she was living. She was convinced that she was acting like a spoiled child, a feeling that was abhorrent to her.

"It's like a black curtain will soon be dropping," she said to Justin.

"It's your imagination, Lib. What could possibly happen to ruin all of this? Seth is doing well. Our health is good. My businesses are thriving."

At 5:13 am. on April 18, 1906, Shorty and Libby were thrown from their bed. Immediately, Libby ran to check on Seth, and returned holding his hand. At his age he was far too big to carry. His eyes were wide with fear, but he wasn't crying.

"Lib, I'm going out to see what's going on."

"It's obviously an earthquake. Please be careful. It's got to be dangerous."

Two hours later Shorty returned dirty and wet to report that fires were raging out of control in many parts of the city due to ruptured gas lines. He told her that the tenements south of Market Street all collapsed when the ground liquefied beneath them, trapping many of the residents inside.

"How horrible. Not too long ago those people were our neighbors. It's only by the grace of God that we were spared."

"Libby, it's not over yet."

With a cracking voice, he told her that Fire Chief Sullivan was killed when the dome of the California Theater and Hotel crashed into his fire station. Most of the telephone and telegraph lines were down.

"Thankfully, the first Army troops from Fort Mason have arrived."

"Is the mayor concerned about looting?

"Definitely."

They moved out on the veranda to study the scene. Roaring fires were everywhere, a conflagration that produced a threatening sky that was both black and red at the same time. The smoke invaded their nostrils and made their bloodshot eyes burn. They noticed a gritty, acrid-bitter taste. It seemed that smoke was swirling everywhere. The sound of fire bells, muffled screams, barking dogs mixed with the incessant roar of the flames. At that moment, another aftershock hit, throwing them both into the far wall.

"I've got to see what I can do to help."

"You'll be killed if you go out there now. I won't let you go."

He agreed to wait until morning. Before eight o'clock he set out again. By mid-afternoon he returned, totally exhausted, his clothes and skin blackened and scorched.

"It's a losing proposition, Lib. City Hall is all but gone. The Winchester Hotel has collapsed. The Hearst Building is ablaze. Mechanics' Pavilion caught fire at about one. St. Mary's Hospital went up a short time later."

"Did the patients get out?"

"Yes. They were loaded onto a ferryboat and taken to Oakland."

"Thank God."

The city looked like a war zone. The entire Financial District behind the Hall of Justice burned. The authorities dynamited buildings to prevent the fire from spreading. The morgue and the police pistol range were crammed with bodies. The mayor issued a decree that any looters would be shot on sight. Libby grew concerned that the fire would reach their home. That night a suspicious fire, probably set by an arsonist, consumed Delmonico's Restaurant, and began creeping its way upward toward Nob Hill. With Shorty assisting, firefighters could not divert it. Meanwhile, the Crocker-Woolworth Bank Building and the St. Francis Hotel at Union Square were lost.

"It's no use, Lib. We've got to get out of here."

"How much time do you think we have?"

"A few hours."

They stood for a moment on the front porch. Even though it was early evening, the sky was black.

"Can't we take some things with us? The piano is priceless. Must we leave it behind to burn? And the paintings—"

"We can't haul those things away without a wagon and horses, and there are none to be had."

"Oh, Justin . . . we'll lose everything."

With difficulty they got to the foot of Van Ness Avenue where officers and crew from the USS *Chicago* were supervising rescue operations. Once on board, they both thanked God for his tender mercies. Young Seth viewed the scene with apparent indifference. Throughout the ordeal he had not spoken a word.

CHAPTER SIX

After the Great Fire, Shorty and Libby settled in Elgin, Illinois, a residential neighborhood located a short distance from Chicago. Tragic memories associated with the recent conflagration in San Francisco eliminated that city as a possibility. Neither had any desire to live in a big city ever again, and Elgin, small as it was, still provided easy access to Chicago after a short commute. Shorty sold his California businesses at a good price, under the circumstances. However, the house and its contents were a total loss with no insurance in place. Thanks to his connections and the proceeds generated from the sale of his former businesses, Shorty reestablished himself. His shipping business on the Great Lakes became the jewel in his crown.

Seth had become a handsome specimen over six feet in height with broad shoulders. His wild-looking, rust-red hair and rubicund complexion provided a rugged appearance enhanced by a physique that was lean and fit from extensive hiking during hunting forays with his stepfather, Justin. Except for the absence of facial hair, he could easily have become what the settlers used to call a mountain man, capable of spending months and years alone in the wild while displaying a grim determination to be as far away from civilization as possible. From age ten on, Seth's foremost desire was to camp, fish and hunt. Firearms had become his passion, and he became a crack shot at an early age.

As time passed, young Seth began to display certain peculiarities. He smiled rarely and spoke infrequently. He preferred to be alone. If forced to socialize, he often chose to antagonize the other children rather than play with them. As Seth aged, the remoteness that he exhibited in his early years didn't dissipate. A debate ensued between Shorty and Libby about what to do regarding his strange behavior, and what to tell him about his lineage.

They were sitting on the veranda; Seth was sleeping in his room. Both Shorty and Libby were wearing robes. Shorty frowned as he looked at her and she ascertained from his expression that he was troubled about something.

"What is it, dear? I can always tell when your motor is racing."

It's not the first time she had read his mind. In addition to being beautiful, Libby was also quite perceptive. Although she was aging, he was convinced that she hadn't lost her beauty or her intelligence.

"You've got to tell him about Soapy Smith," Shorty said. "It's not fair to keep the identity of his father from him."

"But why? Why must we tell him? He thinks you're his father, and you are. You helped raise him. And won't he use that as an excuse for his eccentric behavior?" she asked.

"Maybe so, but he deserves to know. I understand that Smith's family includes many impressive members. You can start by describing Soapy as a black sheep."

Libby followed her husband's advice, telling Seth everything. The words burst out of her.

"Some of Soapy's family members are successful judges, lawyers, and bankers," she said. She also told Seth of his father's brilliance as a crime boss without pulling any punches when describing his criminal ways. As she spoke, she noticed a smile form.

From that day forward, thoughts of Soapy Smith became Seth's obsession. He began to associate his numerous wild impulses with his "evil heritage," as he called it. In his own mind, he was no good, just as his father had been. Worse still, he became convinced that the blood flowing in his veins eliminated any hope of a favorable future. As far as he was concerned, his evil propensities were preordained. Libby saw that her son acted strangely, even more so after learning about Soapy.

After arriving home from school each day, Seth invariably slipped past Libby without speaking on his way to his room. The door would slam shut and he wouldn't emerge until dinner, but only after she yelled for him at least three times at the top of her voice.

Libby was heartsick. They tried counseling but discontinued the sessions after Seth refused to speak. Eventually, she began to regret ever telling him about his real father, but the counselor had insisted it was the right thing to do. At the time, Seth was slightly over six-feet tall with steely blue eyes. Despite his good looks and muscular body, Libby wondered whether his sulky moods and persistent reserve would stifle any chance at romance. Success in business was equally as questionable. Their prayers went unanswered, and Seth's peculiar ways continued. He remained isolated, moody, and curt.

When war erupted in Europe in 1914, Shorty became convinced that he should enlist. He was still young enough and in good shape.

Shorty hesitated to share his thoughts with Libby because he knew what her reaction would be. She would oppose the decision with every fiber of her being. She would remind him of his duty to his family, especially his stepson. Unfortunately, the thought of joining the war effort persisted.

"Libby, the Brits and the French are getting clobbered. The Germans would be in Paris right now but for the miracle on the Marne. The bodies are stacking up. If our allies don't get help soon, they'll lose the war. I've got to get into it."

"What about your businesses? You can't just leave. And what about Seth?"

"Cohen is an excellent second in command. He can hold the fort until I get back. As for Seth, I'll talk to him.""

"The United States isn't in it yet, Darling. You can't go now. It's too early. Besides, you're much too old."

"I am in great shape. And besides, if I wait until that idiot Wilson makes the right decision, it'll be too late. I've got to act now."

"I can't hold you back if you are determined to go but promise me one thing."

"What's that?"

"Promise me that you'll volunteer for the British Medical Corps instead of enlisting in the regular Army."

"Agreed."

After training, Shorty was assigned to the Ypres Salient in Flanders several months after the appointment of Sir Douglas Haig as commander in chief of all British forces. Shorty soon learned that the British had suffered 125,000 casualties (more than 20,000 per month) in the Salient since Haig's appointment, and that the Germans and the French had suffered an equal number of casualties. Even seasoned veterans quaked at orders sending them to the Salient.

Libby went with him to the troop ship unable to hold back tears as she watched her beloved Justin board. Soon enough he arrived at the front and learned quickly that he'd be travelling in a transport caked with mud. The man sitting beside him offered advice.

"When you get to the main trench, the thing to remember is to always keep your head down. There are German snipers everywhere. If you ease up for a second, they'll put a round between your eyes. We've lost twenty or thirty to snipers already. Just yesterday, Thompson took a round in the temple. He never knew what hit him.

A tall man, he forgot to crouch as he adjusted his helmet."

"Sorry to hear about Thompson, but at my height I should be pretty safe," Shorty laughed.

While awaiting orders to move up to the front, Shorty's brigade was assigned to a billet in an abandoned barn and farmhouse a few miles from the front line. In the barn, horse stalls had been removed leaving a large open area with a dirt floor. As Shorty stepped into the large room, a soldier sitting by the door stood.

"How can I help you?"

"I'm Shorty Shaw. They've assigned me to your billet. I'm in the medical unit."

"You're going to be busy, mate. I'll tell you that. I'm Squid and these two reprobates are Wacko and Danforth."

Each man stood and extended a hand.

"How bad is it up here?" Shorty asked.

"Worse than you can imagine," Squid said.

"On the average, the new recruits last about five days," Wacko said.

"Oh, that's encouraging."

"It's the shelling and the incessant sniper fire that have been wiping us out," Danforth said. "We attack and the Germans immediately counterattack. If we push ahead a few miles, the Germans push us back the same distance. Meanwhile, thousands and thousands of men are being killed on each side. They can't bury them fast enough, and the stench has become unbearable, as you've probably already noticed. Dead bodies are everywhere. If you look inside any shell crater, you'll see twisted arms and legs. The wounded ones fight to keep their heads above water, but many drown. Whoever started this war is stark, raving mad."

Shorty would never forget the smell that permeated the atmosphere outside the billet. Human feces combined with decomposing bodies were a putrid stew. Shorty noticed that part of the roof had been blown away on the far side of the room, but the access to fresh air provided no relief from the pungent smell of death.

The men in the room sat in small groups on railroad ties, knapsacks, or other improvised devices. Shorty was told to throw his gear on an upper bunk of a rickety structure at the far side of the room, after which he moved toward his new comrades who were sitting together near the front entrance. He stepped gingerly around and over ammo belts, steel helmets, discarded equipment and sleeping men. Finally, he sat on an empty ammunition case and remained silent, anxious to hear what the men around him were saying.

"The old man is hot to capture Passchendaele Ridge, and he doesn't care how many of us die in the process," Squid said.

"The old man?" asked Shorty.

"Yes. Sir Douglas Haig, a butcher if there ever was one. We've lost so many men under his command that it's difficult to keep count," added Danforth.

"I agree," Squid said. "I think the bastard wants to kill us all. You'll find out soon enough. We've been ordered to move up. Early tomorrow morning our unit will join the main force in the trench up ahead where we'll wait for an hour or so before being ordered over the top. When the time comes, you'll hear a thousand whistles sounding. The medical unit will be expected to follow soon after."

Squid was one of the ugliest men Shorty had ever seen and Wacko was a close second. Squid had a brown spot on his lip caused by overuse of a smoking device, probably a pipe. His face appeared to have been crushed in, even though he insisted that he had never been wounded. Both eyes bulged, adding to his grotesqueness. Wacko had thick eyebrows and deep-socketed, melancholy eyes. His beak of a nose jutted out over thin lips.

"Wait until you meet our rodent army, thousands of the hairy little devils with naked tails and larceny in their hearts. The rats fear nothing. After returning from leave, Samuels from our outfit brought us the biggest stray cat he could find, supposedly to take care of the rats in our trench. The next morning all we found of poor pussy was a tail outside one of the rat holes. All the rest of her had disappeared," said Danforth, whose handsome features were in stark contrast to the appearance of his two comrades.

"No way," Shorty said.

"It's true. And they bite you at night," Wacko said.

"Oh, great. I look forward to that."

"We'll be safe out here from German shelling but as we move forward there'll be no place to hide. If a shell has your name on it, you're dead, simple as that. One place is as good or bad as another. The worst part is being buried alive. By the time they get to you, you're dead from lack of oxygen," Squid said.

"And don't think the enemy will let you off because you're part of the medical corps. No sir. You're as likely to get shelled or shot as the rest of us," Danforth said.

"You guys are so encouraging."

The next morning, October 9, 1914, was the first of several battles near Ypres and focused primarily on Passchendaele Ridge. It had been raining for days, a cold, drenching rain that had turned the battlefield into a stinking quagmire in which horses, dead bodies, heavy equipment, and even wounded men often disappeared. The incessant shelling had turned the area between the opposing trenches into a no-man's land of mud and craters. The rain was unrelenting, and the wind howled. The British artillery unleashed a barrage into the German trenches to precede the attack, but because of the muddy conditions, only about half of the field guns were operable. Worse still, many of the shells wedged into the mud unexploded.

The British troops that were not already in position advanced to the main trench through the communication trenches, a series of deep ditches. When the terrified troops were in place, the order to stand by rattled up the line. Standing in line, Shorty wondered why men were prepared to die in such conditions. *It must be more than just British pluck or love of country.* Whatever the reason, he was convinced that there could never be another war if the pure hell of this one was properly remembered.

Too soon, the shrill scream of the whistles broke forth. Shorty knew that the British attack would center on a small village located a few miles northwest of Passchendaele, and that his medical detail was expected to follow close behind the advancing troops with stretchers at the ready. Soon it became apparent that the Germans had waited to release their full fusillade until the British lines had moved forward some two hundred yards. The eruption of fire into the advancing troops from rifle and machine gun fire and artillery shells was proof that the British barrage had been ineffective. When the fusillade erupted, men begin falling everywhere.

Shorty directed his medical team to prepare to move forward. Once the first two men were up and over, the stretcher that they were to carry was handed up to them. Shorty would never forget the ugly picture of war that presented itself as he pulled himself over the top. Bodies were everywhere, some bloody and still, others writhing in pain because of wounds that would eventually kill them. Many of the wounded had taken cover in shell holes. Shorty spotted one unfortunate soldier inside one and stopped long enough to confirm that the man was beyond help. Thoughts that the enemy would refrain from killing members of the medical team were soon dispelled. Three stretcher bearers were mowed down in front of Shorty, their armbands clearly visible.

By the end of the day, there had been little success at all despite some ten thousand casualties. By then, Shorty and his men had made numerous trips to the field hospital with stretchers carrying the wounded. At the hospital, the doctors worked non-stop to save as many as they could. Shorty was stunned to see the pile of amputated arms and legs reaching to the first sill of the back window of the main aid station.

In one shell crater, Shorty found Danforth covered in mud. An ugly wound in his neck bled profusely. After applying the necessary bandages, Shorty turned to request help from his two aides only to discover that shrapnel from a nearby shell blast had killed them both.

Shorty threw Danforth over his shoulder and began running toward the British aid station. In the process he received a shrapnel wound in the leg that put him out of the war.

CHAPTER SEVEN

Shorty and Libby were sitting together in the den of their large home in Elgin, Illinois. Through the glass of the double doors, they watched the late afternoon sun turning the patio into shadow. The log fire did its best to heat the room, but a chill was present, nonetheless. Sweaters were favored but a shared blanket was also a necessity. They were both resting their legs under the same blanket atop an oversized leather ottoman.

"It was all for naught, Libby. By the time I get Danforth to the aide station he's stone dead. I later learn that Squid and Wacko had suffered the same fate."

"Justin, you can't keep tearing yourself up over this war. You didn't cause it, you can't end it, and you didn't have to enlist. At your age you could have stayed at home. All you get for your trouble is a permanent limp and an ugly scar."

"Lib, I've finally figured it out."

"Figured what out?"

"Why all those men are willing to risk dying. It's because they don't want to let their buddies down."

"Doesn't seem like a proper motivation to me."

"Believe me, it is. But the biggest question relates to the pursuit of war in the first place. Excuse me for being crude, but wars occur because men on both sides want to see who can piss the farthest."

"That is a bit crude, darling, but probably true."

"Older men start wars, and the younger ones are forced to fight them. Old soldiers never die, just the young ones do. And once into it, they do their level best to perform bravely for the sake of their buddies."

"Sounds like a good argument," Libby said.

"It's described as the 'Great War.' I don't see anything *great* about it. With God's help there will never be another. The world can't handle another slaughter like that."

He turned to her.

"Would you like to travel to Europe when the war is over?"

"Oh, yes, I'd love to see Paris."

"Then we'll do it."

Shorty wasn't concerned about leaving his businesses because Bill Cohen had been successfully running them during his absences. Operations had gone smoothly. Thus encouraged, one month after the Armistice, Shorty began to make plans for "the Grand Tour," as he called it. They would start in London, then move on to Paris and Monte Carlo and finally to Rome. Having rented flats in each of the cities for extended periods, Shorty estimated that the excursion would take approximately six months. Unfortunately, one month into the trip Shorty came down with a cold that turned into pneumonia. His doctor insisted that he return home. Back in Elgin, Shorty continued to convalesce after the doctor recommended complete bedrest. Meanwhile, Libby spent more and more time in the office filling in for him. Every evening after dinner she gave her husband a rundown of what happened during the day.

"I don't think Bill Cohen is the trustworthy employee you think he is."

"Why do you say that? He's been handling matters very successfully during my absences. I've placed my complete trust in him. As you know, he's a Harvard business grad who went on to get an MBA at Penn. Now that's a pretty good combination."

"I can't point to anything specific, but I've got a negative feeling about him. Remember my uneasiness before the earthquake and fire. That restlessness turned out to be an accurate precursor of what was about to happen. It's the same feeling I'm having now. Unfortunately, I can't get my hands on the books. He keeps them under lock and key."

"What the hell are you talking about? You're my wife. You're entitled to see everything."

"That's what I told him . . . to no avail."

"You just don't like him, and you haven't liked him from the beginning."

"There's something else. On several occasions he's been visited by shady characters, gangster types. I tried to listen outside the conference room door, but I couldn't hear."

"I'll talk to him tomorrow morning, first thing. It's time for me to get back into the traces anyway."

Shorty showed up unannounced, and was flattered when Marilyn, his trusted secretary, burst into tears of joy upon seeing him. A few people in the office had bet that he would never recover. For Marilyn it was like looking at a resurrected saint. With tears in her eyes, she offered a hug.

"I've missed you, too, Marilyn. Found out how much I hated to be away. Won't do it again. Please ask Mr. Cohen to come see me."

A few minutes later Cohen appeared.

"The world traveler returns. Shorty, I've missed you."

They shook hands, then hugged.

"What's this I hear about your hiding the books?"

"Did Libby tell you that?"

"Of course, and she also told me that certain gangster types have been showing up. What gives?"

"How would you respond if I told you our companies can

generate an extra million dollars a year without any further capital investment?"

"Go on."

"The setup is perfect. We have the vessels to make the shipments, and they have a need to move a particular cargo."

"And the cargo is—"

"Illegal booze . . . out of Canada."

"Are you out of your mind? All we need is to get involved in an illegal liquor operation."

"They came to see us."

"Of course, they did, and once they get their hooks in, they won't let go. How many shipments have there been?"

"One a week for the past four months, but only as an experiment."

"My God! I should fire you. I should fire you on the spot."

"But you won't."

At home that evening, Shorty told Libby about the illegal escapades.

"Why didn't you fire him? You should do it without delay. He's got us involved in an illegal operation. You're going to end up in jail."

"Lib, I've checked the books. Everything is perfect, and like he said, the shipments will produce an extra million a year."

"You can't spend it in jail."

"I'm thinking about you and Seth."

"No, you're not, you're thinking about profits."

"Libby, prohibition is a joke. Booze is flowing as freely as it ever has. The law winks at it and pretends it doesn't exist. The only thing Prohibition has done is empower the criminal element in every major city in the US."

"And you're going to be part of it and find out in the process that they're not nice people. Check the newspapers. There's a murder every other week. I want no part of it. If you move ahead, you move ahead without me."

"You mean you're leaving me over this?"

"I'll stay, but you won't find me in the office from this day forward for any reason."

One week later, Shorty and Cohen met with an underworld figure in Shorty's office. The man, a handsome specimen of average height, in his thirties, and with a slight Italian accent was wearing a pinstriped suit that barely concealed his shoulder holster. He donned a clean white shirt with jeweled cuff links and starched cuffs, a noted contrast to Bill Cohen who was overweight and sloppily dressed. Shorty marveled at the smooth way this young man handled himself.

"I understand you served in Europe," he said.

"I was a volunteer with the British Medical Corps. It was before the U.S. got into it."

"And you received a wound that brought you home . . . we've done our homework."

"I served in the Ypres Salient for a short time before I was wounded."

"You should be proud of your involvement however short it was. One of my cousins fought in the third battle of Ypres. Through him we learned that the battles in the Salient are pure hell."

"It was bad, but you didn't come here today to discuss my war experience."

"No, I didn't. Has Bill filled you in?"

"Yes. If it wasn't for the estimated extra cash, I would give you a negative response right up front and fire him for involving our company in an illegal operation. My wife is convinced we're all going to jail."

"I hate to contradict your wife, but that's absurd," the pinstripe suit said. "Prohibition is a joke. No one takes it seriously. Jail is not a threat, and it never will be."

Cohen piped in. "I recommend that we continue to study the

operation for a few months to see how well it goes. No one will know about this except the three of us. It will be kept totally confidential— no paperwork, no lawyers. Just a handshake."

"I'll agree to that," Shorty said extending his hand.

"My brother should be included as one of the insiders. He couldn't be here today."

"No problem," Shorty said.

CHAPTER EIGHT

When Seth turned eighteen, his world seemed to fall in on him. At the time he was living with his parents at a location not far from Elgin Academy where he attended classes. The school prided itself on being the oldest non-sectarian preparatory school west of the Alleghenies. In Seth's senior year a young woman showed up in history class after the midterm break. He hadn't seen her before. Noting her good looks and obvious intelligence, Seth became smitten, but because of his shyness he made no move to connect with her. Soon Seth learned that she was a member of the Davidson family, which owned the Elgin Bank & Trust Company, the largest bank in town. Her grandfather's recent death had left an opening in the presidency of the bank that her father had filled. She had come to Elgin to live temporarily with her grandmother while her parents found a house and completed the move. Rumor had it that her father had recently contributed a million dollars to the academy.

Though he and Connie lived in the same neighborhood, they were worlds apart socially. The Davidson family was old money with a house three times the size of Seth's. Accordingly, Seth continued to study this young lady from afar, never thinking he might have a chance with her. Then, one day in front of Old Main, it happened.

"Hello," she said. "I'm Connie Davidson."

"Yes . . . I . . . ah . . . know who you are."

"And you're Seth Shaw, am I correct?"

"Yes . . . ah . . . that's me."

"Well, Seth Shaw, I hope you won't think me too bold, but I'd feel honored if you walked me home."

Her interest in Seth wasn't surprising. He was tall, broad-shouldered with a lop-sided grin that made him appear aloof. Unknown to him, he was regarded in some quarters as the best catch on campus, and Connie wanted that prize. They began to meet regularly in front of Old Main after class each day and would walk home together. Connie extended their walks by stopping for ice cream or sitting on a bench by the Fox River until Seth overcame his shyness. Soon, their conversation flowed freely.

Connie complained about being sent to Elgin, which she described as "the end of the world." Their fellow classmates were all stooges, and their teachers were worse, she said. Despite her negative attitude about everything except him, Seth grew increasingly fond of the impeccably dressed girl, who was the envy of her classmates. Connie wore a different scarf every day, and her jeans were pressed. Her favorite shoes apparently were patent leather loafers, which she wore every day. Her hair was bobbed. On her right wrist she wore a charm bracelet, obviously very expensive, that jingled when she moved her arm. There was never a stain or a mark on any of her clothes. She would be in full glory at the school prom and would wear Seth on her arm like another piece of shining jewelry.

"Connie Davidson wants me to take her to the prom, Mom. What do you think?"

"I don't want you to get hurt. The Davidsons are notorious snobs. Her father is a stuffed shirt, and her brother Lowery is worse. I just hope you know what you're doing. Undoubtedly, they see us as *nouveau riche if* they see us at all."

"I know about all of that. I don't intend to marry her. I'm just taking her to the prom. Besides, I volunteered to help set up for prom night. So now I get to go with the prettiest girl in school."

"Be careful. That's all I have to say."

Seth bought a new suit and shoes for the occasion with money given him by Shorty. He also asked his father for the car, a request that to his surprise was promptly granted.

To save him embarrassment, his mother purchased a corsage and had it waiting for him in the refrigerator on prom day. After dinner, Seth put on his new suit and studied himself in the mirror. The suit fit perfectly, but the shiny patent leather shoes caused pain from the moment he puts them on.

When he got to Connie's house, he pulled the car into the circular driveway, and walked slowly toward the front door. Lowery waited for him at the end of the walk.

"Where do you think you're going?"

Lowery was the type of snob you'd expect to see in jodhpurs and high riding boots at a fox hunt. He wore a jersey with red and white stripes and white pants. His blond hair covered one side of his face. His thin moustache gave him a sinister look that contrasted greatly with his squeaky voice.

"I've come to pick up your sister. I'm taking her to the prom."

"I don't think so. You're nothing but white trash in a big house."

Seth stopped in his tracks. "I'm telling you right now, if you make one more negative comment about my family, I'm going to thrash you."

"Your father can have as many businesses as he wants, but in the end he's still an outlander."

Seth lunged at Lowery, dropping to one knee, and grabbing Lowery's leg, and dropping him to the ground. Seth stood over Lowery and kicked his face, knocking out four of his front teeth and causing an eruption of blood. Lowery was out cold. Seth added one last touch by stuffing the corsage intended for Connie into his mouth.

As he walked to his car, Seth noticed that his suit pants were ripped at the knee, and at that moment he vowed that he would never again reach above his status for the sake of a woman. As far as Connie Davidson was concerned, such restraint wasn't necessary.

She would never again speak to him.

The next day Shorty called him into the study.

"What on earth happened? All hell has broken loose. Young Lowery is in the hospital. His father said he would be there for at least four days. He'll need plastic surgery and a bridge. The man is livid. Even when I offered to pay all expenses, he didn't cool. He refuses to take my money."

Shorty stopped pacing and turned to face Seth.

"Davidson is so angry he plans to use his influence with Elgin Academy to have you expelled. What do you have to say for yourself?"

"I won't apologize. He blocked my way. Then he called you an *outlander*, whatever that means. The implication is that our family's low status prevents me from dating his sister. My anger got the best of me. I went over the top, I know, but I couldn't hold back. I wanted to kill him."

"What caused you to act so viciously?"

Seth knew the answer; he had inherited his explosive temper from his biological father, Soapy Smith.

"Let's just say that I felt the fury of my ancestors. It may have been excessive, but it is a force that has been passed down to me."

"Don't give me that bullshit!" Shorty said. "Soapy Smith died long ago, and the best thing you can do now is to let him stay buried."

Seth turned to leave. "By the way," his father said. "Thanks for defending me."

A week later, Seth was called into the headmaster's office. Horace Fox was not the kind of man students in a small private school, or any school, admired. A blowhard of the first order, he acted as if his graduation from Yale was the only accomplishment in life he would ever need. Most unattractive of all was his practice of fawning over rich alumni and important contributors. Seth knew what awaited. Lowery was a graduate of Elgin, and his father had recently contributed a bundle.

"Mister Shaw sit down . . . over there. There are serious charges being lodged against you. Percival Tolliver tells us that you have stolen money in the prom fund, an amount exceeding two hundred dollars," the headmaster said.

"If he said that, he's a liar."

"On the contrary, he tells us that he saw you do it."

"I don't know anything about that fund, and certainly never had access to it. I'm not even on the committee. I was just a volunteer to help set up for the dance."

"Come on, Mister Shaw, we've got you dead to rights."

"Not so, because I didn't do it."

"This is quite annoying. The faculty and the Board of Trustees are hoping that you'll save us the trouble of setting up a Board of Inquiry. If that is what you'd prefer, then that's what you'll get. You're dismissed"

As Seth stood in front of Old Main, he felt his anger rising. It was obvious that he was being set up, and there was no doubt in his mind who was behind it.

It's Old Man Davidson! He wants to make sure that I'm disgraced. When he's through with me, no college in the land will accept me.

At that moment he remembered that Tolliver, his accuser, was a boarder.

"Tolliver! I'm coming in."

Seth opened the door and entered. Because Tolliver had elected to room alone, his quarters were extremely small. Aside from a bed, desk and bureau, there was not much furniture. Sitting at his desk, Tolliver had a look of pure terror when he saw Seth barge in.

"Don't hurt me, Seth. You'll just make it worse."

"Who put you up to this, you little bastard. You know perfectly well that every word of your story is an outright lie. Are you willing to tell me what is going on or do I have to break your arm to find out?"

"No, no, don't do that."

Resigned, Tolliver stood from his desk and removed his eyeglasses. As Seth stepped toward him, Toliver quivered.

"All right all right. But I've got to tell you that I'll deny ever talking to you. I must. My father's job is at stake. He works for Davidson. If I don't pin this on you, my father's job is history. Without it my family is in the poorhouse. Old man Davidson has assured my father that he'll never work again if I don't pull this off."

"So that's it."

"Yes, that's it. You're the patsy, and all the pieces are in place. Of course, your attack on Lowery is behind it all. I understand you beat the shit out of him. You've got to understand, man, that there are no hard feelings on my part. There is nothing else I can do."

Seth left, fists clenched in anger. As he walked past Old Main on his way across campus, he felt his throat growing tight, as though someone was strangling him. For a few seconds, he considered murdering old man Davidson, or Lowery, or both. But then he thought better of it. Such revenge wasn't worth a life in prison, and he knew the Davidson wouldn't settle for anything less.

Two days later, Seth jumped a freight heading south without informing his parents where he was going and with very little money. When he told Tolliver what he intended to do, Tolliver slipped him a hundred dollars, in part to ease his guilty conscience.

CHAPTER NINE

The trip from Chicago to New Orleans was unpleasant. Each freight car Seth rode in was dirty, damp, cramped, and in most cases, occupied by drunks and vagrants. Back at home, his parents were devastated by his sudden departure. Seth's brief note explained that he loved his parents and fled to protect them and himself from the Davidsons.

Early on in his travels, Seth befriended a man named Keano, who was heading south in the same freight car. Skin dark, and arms like tree trunks, Keano had a thick neck and shiny head, and at six-foot-six stood a head taller than Seth. He was clean-shaven and ruggedly handsome, with knife scars on his chin and cheeks. Shoeless, he wore stained, grey trousers rolled up at the bottom and a T-shirt with no sleeves.

Between the two of them, they arranged for one to play watchdog while the other slept. The other stowaways gave them both a wide berth. During the long journey there was plenty of time to think. For the most part, Keano refused to be drawn into conversation. Seth would sit for hours without saying a word, legs drawn up and chin on knees. He was transfixed by the rhythm of the car. When he looked through the open door, he could see unchanging farmland interspersed with herds of cattle and horses, flocks of sheep, and bright yellow haystacks. The monotony added to his dark mood. The wooden floor of the boxcar was covered with mud that was black with oil, grease, and excrement, the smell leaving no doubt as to its origin. Unfortunately, the stifling air added to the odiferous intensity. What little air there was, leaked in through the few missing wooden planks in the side walls. At times, the air was so hot and humid that Seth felt as if he might pass out. It got more oppressive as their southbound journey neared its destination—New Orleans.

"Why New Orleans?" Keano asked during a rare instance of affability.

"Why not?" Seth answered.

Keano answered with a grunt. Seth continued.

"You're the expert. I don't suppose this car will carry us all the way."

"No Suh, two, maybe three transfahs. Juss watch me. Ah been heah afore."

"Agreed.""

Seth returned to his funk.

"You've got *the black dog*," Keano said.

"Pardon?"

"Pappy calls it *the black dog*. Causes his crazy moods."

"Is it that obvious?"

"Like tits on a rattlesnake."

Seth felt oddly reassured to learn that he wasn't alone in his suffering.

"Got my oldest brother, too. One moment he's all powerful, a god on earth. The next, he's squashed like a bug. There's a rage that comes with it, too."

"What happened to your brother?"

"Lynched him. Klan got no stomach for Black boys with powerful thoughts."

"I'm sorry."

Keano nodded, then became silent again. Two days later, Keano was shaking Seth awake.

"Come on, boy, we comin' up on the city yards. Gotta jump befo the bulls arrive. They got clubs."

The other occupants had already departed. With one springing leap Seth was out of the car, carpetbag in hand, down a steep slope, through high grass. Keano led, holding his battered bag above his head, both stopping abruptly at the bottom.

"You hurt?" Keano asked.

"No. What in blazes are we going to do now?" Seth asked.

"Simple. Carl, ma brudda . . . he works at the Rising Sun. Best chippy-house in da city."

"Chippy-house?"

"Cat house, brothel, home for soiled doves. It be run by Missy Claudette. Lotta folks thinks dat Storyville heah in New Orleans be de place to go for de bes white pussy. Jus ain't so. Missy Claudette, she gots de bes talent, and her place ain't no crib, no sah. It be an elegant parlor house, 'bout as far from a brothel for coloreds as you can get."

"What would a madam in a place like that possibly want with the likes of us?"

"Gets rowdy in dem places at times. Dey ken always use notha set of powerful fists, dats sure. My brudda makes me look like limp toast."

They stopped off at a local gas station to freshen up. The sign on the bathroom door—*No Blacks Allowed*—brought home that they were in a different world. Rather than upstage his friend, Seth followed Keano to a stream out back where they both cleaned themselves as best they could.

Later Seth brought food from a local diner. An hour later they approached the Rising Sun, feeling somewhat clean and relatively presentable. As they stood outside the back door, Keano sent word to his brother. When Carl appeared, there was a lot of whooping and hand slapping—high, low, behind the back and so forth—with screams of pleasure. Carl was a carbon copy of Keano, only larger and darker, both with trunk-like arms and bulging chests.

"Don't be thinkin you ken thrash dis black ass," Carl would say.

Whereupon Keano would respond, "Why you sombitch, I'll fold you like a pretzel."

It was obvious they loved each other deeply. In fact, they got so enthusiastic and made so much noise that Madam Claudette popped her head out of an upstairs window.

"Carl, what on earth is going on out there?"

"Missy Claudette, dis here be my brudda, who I ain't seen in three long yars. And this here be his fren, Seth."

"Welcome, gentlemen." She moved onto a balcony. All three smiled up at her. "I would ask you to keep it down out there. Several girls are working," she said.

"Missy Claudette, both dese men, dey wants jobs," Carl said.

"We can use them. If they're as helpful as you have been, Carl, they'll be worth their wages."

"Why, thank you, Missy Claudette."

Aside from the flame-red lipstick and glittering fingers showing expensive rings, one on each finger, there was nothing in the plain black dress and black shoes and modest hairdo that would reveal her profession. Slightly overweight, but not excessively so, she appeared to be in her mid-forties. Her smile was porcelain perfect. Looking for a hardness that wasn't there, Seth saw instead a grace that seemed out of place somehow.

"Here are the rules. You can work out the schedule with the others, but I'll want at least two of you here twenty-four hours a day with one day off a week. Keep in mind that you're to use the back door at all times when going and coming, the one over there." She pointed.

"You'll both be given clothes to wear—white shirt, black suit and tie, black shoes—all provided by me. I'll also furnish you with a firearm, black socks, and underwear. The House will clean your clothes, but you've got to bring the items to me when they're ready to be washed. After you're here a week you'll get a second set of clothes."

She paused and studied the newcomers.

"Your wages will be eight dollars a week plus tips. Is that agreeable?

"Yes Ma'am," they answered in unison.

"I don't provide room and board for Blacks, but this young man here can stay inside," she said, pointing to Seth. "You all will be given one meal a day, either lunch or dinner. You choose." She paused. "Carl, your brother will have to find his own lodgings."

"Thas okay, Missy Claudette. Keano he be staying wid me."

It didn't take Seth long to get the lay of the land. The gigantic brothel had many rooms—sleeping accommodations in one wing and rooms for assignation in the other. Seth's room was behind the furnace in the basement. Fifteen ladies worked the House, which was famous throughout the South for its hot, beautiful women and fine ambiance. There were other houses in New Orleans, but none with the quality of experience offered at the Rising Sun, such things as silk sheets changed three times a night, clean rooms, and an all-pervading elegance.

Madam Claudette ensured that all aspects of the operation ran smoothly. There was one open area known as the living room where ladies not currently engaged gathered. Whereas other establishments exhibited their girls in such places in flimsy outfits, Madam Claudette insisted that all her flock be properly attired, preferably in robes. Miss Claudette referred to her girls as *boarders*. All were elegantly clad. No drugs were permitted on the premises. Madam Claudette never missed an opportunity to brag that some of her best clients were respectable members of society. Rumor had it that the mayor and the governor frequently attended.

Madam Claudette took an immediate shine to Seth. As the years progressed, she kept advancing his position until he was head of security. Although there was no sexual connection between them, everyone assumed otherwise because of her affection toward him. She never failed to call Seth "Honey" and hugged him whenever they passed each other in one of the hallways. Seth's duties were essentially administrative unless Madam Claudette gave him a special assignment.

Beginning at three each afternoon, the pianist, dubbed the Professor, would arrive ready to play until three in the morning, always wearing a bowler hat and an old sport jacket too small for his tall and lanky frame. During his shift, the ladies would accost him with special requests that ranged from Scott Joplin and Stephen Foster to Mozart. Many of the regular patrons had favorites they would also request, and the Professor was expected to remember the preferences of the brothel's most frequent and best customers.

Seth soon discovered that some of the ladies were insatiable. After working all day, they often appeared at his door at night. Occasionally, two would arrive at once, ready to invent new ways of lovemaking. Given the expertise of his enthusiastic partners, Seth learned things that he'd never even considered. Of all the ladies who visited him, Bessie was the most notable. He thoroughly enjoyed their frolics late at night and came to know her special knock. At the same time, he wondered how he could descend into such debauchery without guilt. At such times, he remembered that he was descended from an unscrupulous man, blaming his bloodline for his immoral tendencies.

"Do you think Claudette knows about us?" Seth asked Bessie.

"Sure enough. I told her some time ago," Bessie laughed.

"And she doesn't mind . . . ?"

"Why should she mind? So long as we girls service the customers in a way that brings them back, that's all she cares about."

When America entered the Great War in 1918, a patriotic spirit surged through New Orleans. Parading troops became commonplace. Seemingly, the stars and stripes waved from all windowsills and flagpoles. Like many of the men his age, Seth became caught up in the frensy.

"Miss Claudette, I want to serve my country."

"Of course. How old are you?"

"Eighteen."

"A mere pup. You're willing to risk dying, and you haven't even started to live yet. You're a brave boy."

"Thank you."

"I suppose you want a leave of absence?"

"Yes, ma'am."

"Why don't we wait until you've passed your physical? After all, you could have flat feet," she laughed.

Later, an Army doctor gave him the bad news.

"You have a social disease."

"Say it in plain words, Doc."

"You've got gonorrhea. Comes from sticking your pipe in the wrong sewers."

"Oh."

Maybe the Rising Sun isn't a special paradise after all, he mused.

"What are the symptoms?"

"Well, for one thing, pain during urination and intercourse."

"Anything else?"

"Occasional discharge."

"You're right, Doc. I've got it. What do we do now?"

"You can't sign up until you're cured, but don't despair. I'll give you pills that should clear things up. I'm also giving you a prescription. They'll be refills to last you three months. That should be long enough."

"You mean it'll take three months to get rid of it?"

"At least, maybe longer."

"Doc, I don't want to miss this war."

Seth considered informing Miss Claudette of his trouble, but Keano advised against it, using strong language to make his point. The most likely action on her part, he said, would be to "throw your ass out." The better course, he said, was to wait for the cure and tell her then.

"In the meantime, you got to stay buttoned up."

Seth counted each pill to make sure he was doing it right. At the end of the third month, he went back to the recruiting office. No trace was found. By the time Seth got the okay, it was September.

Following basic training, Seth went immediately to sniper school, but before being sent overseas, the war ended. After his honorable discharge, he returned to New Orleans and commiserated with Keano.

"Hey, don't be sad. Dat dose couda saved yo life," Keano said. "Lotsa guys died over theya."

"How'd you get to stay out of it?"

"Flat feet."

They both laughed.

Soon after his return, Madam Claudette told Seth that Blackie Condron, one of the most notorious gangsters in New Orleans at the time, would be arriving Friday night. His expected arrival was creating quite a stir. She called all security personnel together.

"I want all of you to be here Friday night," Claudette said. "Blackie is notorious for getting ugly when he drinks, and he'll be bringing a truckload of goons with him who are just as bad."

"Who's the lucky girl?" Seth asked.

"It's always Bessie."

Blackie arrived dressed to the nines in a dark-blue suit, three-piece, with white spats, a pink carnation in his lapel and a white handkerchief in his breast pocket. A pink dress-shirt and a wide yellow tie completed the ensemble. His black hair, oily and shiny, was slicked strait back, his mustache thin and well-kept. He moved like a ballet dancer with yellow gloves to confirm the image.

"Ah, Claudette, it's been a long time."

"Too long, Blackie. Bessie's waiting for you upstairs in the usual room. I took the liberty of providing champagne and caviar."

"Did you remember the oysters?"

"I certainly did. It's all waiting for you."

"You're too kind my lady. I thank you," he said bowing.

By then, the Professor, playing piano in the parlor, switched to *Mary's A Grand Old Name* by George Cohan, Blackie's favorite tune. As Blackie climbed the stairs to the second floor, three goons quickly followed with three girls in tow. An hour later, Blackie appeared at the top of the stairs, but the three goons were not there to greet him. *Curious,* he thought. Once again, the Professor switched to the Cohan favorite, but as Blackie hit the third stair in his descent, the music abruptly stopped. The Professor stood up and calmly pulled a revolver out from under the piano lid. His first shot missed Blackie, who, for some reason, stood frozen and weaponless. Even as the Professor moved forward to get a better shot, Blackie didn't move.

The Professor didn't get a second chance. From the far side of the room, Seth stepped forward, pistol drawn. Blackie heard a shot, and when he looked down, he saw a large hole in the back of the Professor's head.

Madam Claudette appeared, animated and yelling. "This didn't happen. And none of you observed it. Do you all understand that? Thankfully, it's a marble floor which will clean easily. After that, we'll dispose of the body. Put him in a burlap sack full of rocks and dump him in the river. I don't want any police investigation, and that means that everyone must button lip. Do we all understand?"

They all nodded.

"Now get to work."

Blackie moved from his position on the stairs.

"Who is it that saved my life, Claudette?"

"Seth Shaw," Claudette answered, pointing.

"Seth Shaw, I'm forever in your debt. You saved my life with great shooting. You certainly know what you're doing. If you hadn't stepped in, I'd be singing with the Heavenly Choir right now. If there's anything I can do for you ever you let me know."

"It was a lucky shot."

"The hell it was, lad. You just remember what I said."

Two of Claudette's bouncers carried the body out of the room while Keano and Seth began cleaning up the blood.

"I don't carry a gun, makes my suits look lumpy," Blackie said.

He paused, then looked at Claudette. "Claudette, who was it tried to kill me?

"His name is Pat Murray, better known as the Professor. Been playing for me for three months. I expect that a rival boss got to him. Must have offered a lot of money. He's a loser and a loner. No family at all."

"Claudette, how do I know that you didn't set me up?"

"Come on, Blackie. The finger points back at you. Why did your three goons disappear? Why, if I had planned it, would I have assigned my best men to the security detail?"

When one of the girls checked upstairs, the three goons were gone, confirming Claudette's suspicion of an inside job. All three were discovered later floating in the river, evidence of Blackie's swift revenge. A week later, the local police inspector requested that Claudette meet him at a secure location in the Latin Quarter.

"Claudette, I owe you a lot. You pay me well. However, I'm getting incredible pressure to investigate an alleged murder that supposedly occurred at your establishment a few days ago. It seems your piano player was queer. His boyfriend is raising all sorts of hell. He said someone at your place killed his lover."

"Charlie, I—"

"Don't implicate yourself, Claudette. Just be silent until I've finished. I'm just speaking hypothetically, but if there's a person who just might have killed the piano player, because the piano player is a paid assassin hired to kill Blackie Condron, then it might be a good idea for that young man to get the hell out of town."

"I get the message, Charlie, and I appreciate the tip."

"Yes, and it might be a good idea to send him on his way very quickly because the roommate is threatening to go to the press if my boys don't investigate right away. And Claudette—"

"Yes?"

"Speaking hypothetically, if the body of the piano player is thrown in the river in a bag full of rocks, within a week there won't be anything left, and an investigation usually gets sidetracked when a body isn't found."

He smiled slyly at Claudette as they both stood to leave.

"You're saying this should blow over?"

He kept smiling but said nothing further.

CHAPTER TEN

A s she walked toward Blackie's office, Claudette marveled at the accuracy of police informants. She had arrived at the Condron Building and passed through the main entrance. As a front, Blackie had set up what appeared to be a legitimate real estate company. The receptionist gave a look that made Claudette know she was aware of Claudette's profession. Noting the sneer, Claudette lost her nerve.

"I've decided not to bother him at his office."

As she turned to leave, she heard Blackie's voice.

"Claudette . . . come right on in."

The office was tastefully done in satin green wallpaper. Around the room were large paintings of ships, most in full sail. Directing her to a large leather chair, Blackie sat in an identical chair beside her.

"What can I do for you, Claudette?"

"May I speak freely?"

"Of course."

"I just finished a conversation with Charlie."

"You mean our esteemed chief inspector?"

"The very same. He's getting nervous. Turns out the Professor had a sweet roommate, and this guy is pressing for an investigation."

"You don't say."

"Not only that, but this same guy is threatening to go to the press, which Charlie said could bring discomfort to us all."

"What does Charlie suggest?"

"Well, he can dance through the motions of an investigation which will get nowhere without a body. In the meantime, he suggests that we get the kid out of town."

"The kid?"

"Yeah, Seth Shaw, the young man who saved your life."

"Oh, yes, I agree totally. I'll take care of it. Send him to me."

A day later Seth appeared in Blackie's office.

"My God, boy, what's happened to you?"

"You mean the nose. I was on duty last night when some toughs appeared. They went after my friends, Carl and Keano, so I got into it."

"And one of the toughs broke your nose."

"Exactly."

"Those friends, are black?"

"Yeah, so what?"

"You're telling me that you went to the aide of two Negroes?"

"Sure. They're my friends. I didn't think twice about it."

"Well, you paid for it."

"I guess so."

"Your nose is slapped sideways. You should get it reset as soon as possible. I want you to go to see Doc Wycoff. I'll pay for all expenses, and I'll make sure he fits you in this afternoon."

"Thanks," Seth said.

"There's one other thing."

"What's that?"

"You've got to get out of town . . . and fast. I've arranged for transportation. Your train leaves tomorrow morning. Be sure to be on it. Here's the ticket. I've also decided to have you connect with the Simboli family in Chicago. Carlos is a good friend of mine. The address is on this sheet of paper."

Seth left Doc Wycoff's office late afternoon. His nose, now straightened, was in a splint held in place with white tape. Walking through the back door of the Rising Sun, he perceived that something terrible had happened. Bessie and several other girls were sobbing.

"What's happened?" Seth asked.

"Where've you been?" Bessie asked.

"Never mind that, just tell me what's happened."

"They came for Carl and Keano. Must've been twenty of them . . . wearing hoods. Instead of hiding, Keano and Carl got out there to meet them. They were overpowered. There's nothing we could do."

She stopped to catch her breath.

"It was horrible. They got two ropes . . . said they were gonna make them pay. They dragged Carl and Keano down to the river."

"Did you follow them?"

"We're too scared for that. Those maniacs are screaming and shouting and pounding those poor boys with poles."

"Bessie, please get a message to the police and the coroner immediately," Seth said.

Bessie nodded and ran off.

Carl and Keano were hanging from two separate limbs of a gigantic tree. After cutting the bodies down, Seth had several minutes to wait before the coroner arrived. *How can something like this happen in America?* Seth was certain that the pain he felt would be the same if he'd lost members of his immediate family. His hands shook and vision blurred. These men had befriended him, showed him kindness. And he wasn't there to help them. Worse still, because of his travel plans, he would be unable to attend their funerals. Tragically, he must rely on Claudette to convey his condolences.

Waiting for the authorities, he looked down at the two bodies strewn on the grass in front of him, naked and exposed, their arms folded across each chest. *How peaceful they look.* He steadied himself against the tree, concerned that he might pass out and topple over. So many forces were at play—guilt, anger, remorse, terror, disappointment—that he felt the black curtain of depression taking hold. His vision blurred again, and he felt off balance.

That night in his bedroom Seth put his feelings onto paper. With pencil and a blank sheet of paper, he began to write with the faint assistance of a nearby candle:

LYNCHING
As a young boy
I'm forced to watch.
Look there, my father said.
See what we do to niggers.
A young man,
no older than my sister
dangles from a rope
slowly turning, turning,
his skin black from pigment
and from burning.

Years later,
my father safely dead,
I return
to that infamous spot.
The gnarled tree is free
of any marks,
but the mind-corpse
will forever be
turning, turning,
refusing to rot.

He extinguished the light and lay wide-eyed unable to sleep. *Where does the inspiration for my writing come from?* Just before his eyes closed the answer came to him. *The Black Dog!*

When he took his seat on the train the next morning, his

throbbing nose added to his black mood. The seats in the passenger car were blue leather showing very little wear. The interior was obviously of recent vintage showing wood paneling and overhead globes. Even so, second class couldn't compete with the floor rugs, hanging chandeliers, and clustered seating that was offered in first class. Seth's car had rows of seating on each side of the aisle. Travel snobs would compare such layouts to subway cars, but Seth was content. In his assigned seat, Seth slid his bowler down close to his eyes as a signal that he didn't want to talk to anyone. The ploy didn't work. The passenger in the seat across the aisle leaned in close.

"What the hell happened to you?" the man asked.

"You mean my nose. Walked into a door," Seth said.

"Happened to me once. The splint holds the bone steady and protects against further fractures. The white tape holds the splint in place," the stranger said.

"That's about it," Seth said, his lip curling slightly.

"You're a sight to behold, I'll tell you that."

"I don't plan to enter any beauty pageants."

"How long you got to look like that?"

"At least three weeks," Seth said.

"Poor boy."

The man wore checked trousers, a dark high-buttoned sack coat, a colorful tie, and a vest over a white shirt with a rounded collar. Judging from the rakish angle of the straw porkpie hat, Seth suspected he was something of a dandy, and no older than forty.

"My name's Brandon Smithers," he said.

Seth considered moving his seat, but the car was filled. The few women on board wore bonnets, and most of the men favored bowlers. Considering the high temperature in the car, Seth was struck by the fact that most men were wearing jackets and white shirts. Sadly, the high windows offering splendid views of the outside scenery could not be opened because of the dust, cinders and debris that would inevitably blow through. Seth noticed a young girl three seats up wearing a large straw hat leaning into the aisle despite her mother's attempts to hold her back.

Seth turned his attention back to Smithers.

"I'm Seth Shaw," he answered reluctantly.

They shook hands. "I'm Brandon."

"Look, Brandon, I'm not much in the mood for—"

"I'm headed for Chicago. How 'bout you?"

"Same," Seth said.

"Say, do you know what an NDE is?' Brandon asked.

"Can't say as I do."

"It stands for *Near Death Experience.* I work for a professor named Theodore Mansfield. He's doing studies of NDEs here in the States. He sends me out to interview people who've had them. I take notes that he uses in his study."

"Why doesn't he go himself?" Seth asked.

"He's disabled in a wheelchair. Needs me to do the grunt work and I've got the background to do it. Worked some years for the Pinkertons."

"How does he find these people?"

"Newspapers. He reads as many as he can find. Also, he has connections with some of the largest hospitals."

"How many NDEs have you interviewed so far?" Seth asked.

"'Bout fifty. It's uncanny. All the experiences are essentially the same."

"What do you mean by 'essentially the same?'" Seth asked.

Smithers reached for a battered leather satchel in the overhead.

"Let me read from some of my notes so that I don't miss anything."

He sat, pulled out papers from the satchel, and began to read.

"'The subject states that what he has experienced cannot be expressed in human language. He hears himself declared dead. He no longer feels pain and is perfectly relaxed. Having left his body, he begins to float in a way that permits him to observe what is happening around him. He is sucked into a sort of tunnel where deceased family members are waiting for him. He perceives a brilliant light. He relives his life in the smallest detail. He comes up against a kind of frontier and finds himself back in his body.'"

"And many of the reports are essentially the same, according to you?" Seth asked.

"Pretty much. Let me give you an example. I'm returning from interviewing a young girl and her family in New Orleans. Little Beth who is seven-years-old falls into a swimming pool and drowns. When they fish her out, there is no sign of cardiac or cerebral activity. That condition remains for nineteen minutes. As you may know, that is very unusual. After three minutes of clinical death the brain cells stop functioning for lack of oxygen. Within ten minutes large areas of the brain have turned into sieves. Yet, after almost twenty minutes after she is pulled from the water she recovers. Keep in mind that there has been heart stoppage, a flat electro-encephalogram and respiratory arrest."

"Go on," Seth said.

"In spite of all that, she awakens and shows no after-effects"

"Impossible," Seth said.

"You'd think so, yet she talks freely about her experience. She tells me that a guardian angel took her on a journey. At the end of it she met her Eternal Father who asked her if she wanted to go back. At first, she told him she wanted to stay. Then, she reversed herself when told that her mother was crying. Instantaneously, she was in her body again."

"It can't happen. There must be drugs involved or something similar," Seth said

"No evidence of drugs. After all, Beth was a child, not even eight years old at the time."

"Well, something else must be going on," Seth said.

Smithers removed a handful of pages from his satchel.

"Let me read to you from some other testimonials. Mind you, these quotes are taken directly from the lips of many different subjects, not just Beth. Here's one. 'I took a trip to heaven. I saw the most beautiful lakes. Angels—they were floating around like you see seagulls. Everything was white. The most beautiful flowers. Nobody on this earth ever saw the beautiful flowers that I saw there.'"

Smithers fumbles through his papers.

"Here's another," he said. "*'Inside I saw what appeared to be a street of golden color with an overlay of glass or water. The yellow light that appeared was dazzling. There is no way to describe it. I saw no figure, yet I was conscious of a person. Suddenly I knew the light was Jesus, the person was Jesus.'*"

"And this one," Smithers said. "'We sat side by side on a rock, overlooking the most beautiful landscape I had ever seen. The colors were outside my experience, vivid beyond my dreams, the composition exceptional. It was exceptionally pleasant and there was no pressure, for my friend knew me and loved me more than I could know or love myself. I had never felt such radiance and peace.'"

"Here's another," Smithers said. "'The subject suddenly finds himself out of his body, floats up to the ceiling and observes what is happening around his physical envelope. This seems perfectly reasonable to him, and he feels no pain. If the patient is suffering from some physical infirmity (myopia for example), it disappears . . . he feels himself sucked at extraordinary speed into a tunnel at the end of which he sees a light beckoning him on.'"

"Again, a light," Seth said.

"Yes, a light," Smithers said. He continued to read from his notes. "'The closer he comes to it, the more he wants to merge with it. That light is described as being stronger than a thousand suns at their zenith. His whole life passes before him like a film, in the space of ten seconds, fusion with the light, a dialogue with the Light Being, who ends by saying, 'Your hour has not yet come; you must return and finish your job.' Sometimes the subject is asked, 'Do you wish to stay here or return?'"

"Here's another," Smithers said. "'I traveled through the tunnel at unbelievable speed. I met three beings of light. And I knew they were angels. Then I found myself really in the white light, that everybody talks about, that envelops you with infinite love, so every atom of your being quivers with passionate love. It was so marvelous. Words can't express what I felt."

"Listen to this one from a child," Smithers said. "'A woman named Elizabeth appeared, and the tunnel became bright. The woman was tall with bright yellow hair. She stated that, 'Heaven was fun. It was bright and there were lots of flowers.'"

"That same child said some very interesting things," Smithers said. "She said that there was a border around heaven that she could not see past. She said that she met many people, including her dead grandparents, her dead maternal aunt and Heather and Melissa, two adults waiting to be reborn. She then met the 'heavenly Father and Jesus.'"

"Hold on, she said that she met 'the heavenly Father *and* Jesus.' She's describing God and Jesus as two separate entities," Seth said.

"Yes."

"Well, that will certainly make the prelates jump out of their slippers. And think about it. Have you every counted the obituaries for one city alone. Hundreds of them every week. Then multiply that by the number of cities in the U.S. Or think of the number of people dying each day throughout the world or the number who have died since we started counting. If each subject gets a special greeting, the Big Guy's going to be awfully busy. Something else is going on. Keep talking."

"My boss asked the same questions and so do I. Yet, the testimonials keep coming. Here's another. 'And deep within me came an instant and wondrous recognition. I, even I, was facing God.'

"One subject asked questions about the sufferings of his people. 'He comes away with the conviction that there is a reason for everything that happens, no matter how awful it appears in the physical world.'" Smithers said. "Heaven is a different matter altogether as one subject notes. 'There are beautiful flowers there. I was with God and Jesus.'"

"I've heard enough," Seth said.

"Wait, you still haven't heard about interventions," Smithers said.

"Interventions?"

"I'm sure you've heard the stories. Soldiers in wartime hear a voice that said, 'Move to a new location right away.' The subject moves and seconds later a shell hits, killing every man in the prior location. That's an intervention—God, or Jesus or a guardian angel, or an outside force, depending on the account, gives a warning just in time."

"And I suppose you've got many testimonials regarding this," Seth said.

"Yes, many."

"Look, Brandon, I'd like to hear about them, but—"

"WHAT HAPPENED TO YOUR NOSE, MISTER?"

It was the little girl with the oversized straw hat standing in the aisle in front of Seth.

"Some bad men tried to beat me up. They broke my nose in the fight."

"What happened to the bad men?"

"I don't know. Unfortunately, I had to leave town on urgent business before I could hit them back."

"You ran away," she said over her mother's shoulder as she was scooped up and returned to her seat.

Smithers seemed confused by Seth's revised description of what happened to his nose.

"I thought you said—"

"You can't lie to a kid. They're too smart for that," Seth said.

Smithers pretended to look out the window, avoiding further conversation, giving Seth a chance to sleep the rest of the way.

Despite the wad of money in his pocket given to him by Madam Claudette, when Seth reached Chicago, he decided to stay in an inexpensive boardinghouse on Polk Street, west of Vernon Park near the hospital. He told the landlady, Emma Parkinson, that he planned to be there for only a few days until he found a well-paying job.

Emmie had seen boarders come and go over the years, but Seth Shaw was something special. *This one will amount to something,* she thought. She noted that he was well-spoken and intelligent with the type of rugged good looks her daughter had always favored, enhanced by a bandaged nose showing his toughness in an altercation he wouldn't discuss. *If only Sandra hadn't married.*

In the morning, Seth went downstairs to find Emmie in the kitchen. She was wearing a checkered robe that reached her ankles, her brown, graying hair disheveled. Years past she may have been pretty, but the onset of middle age had removed any semblance of that. He was glad for the opportunity to talk with her and wished he had more time to kill before his eleven o'clock appointment. The other boarders were all early risers who had gone off to work.

"Alcohol is choking this city. The demand for bootleg booze has reached astronomical levels," Emmie said while picking up breakfast plates and putting them in the sink.

"Night life in Chicago is erupting. On any given night, convertibles, and cabs full of revelers can be seen speeding along the streets searching for the best speakeasies, the ones that offer high-grade booze and no closing hours. A party atmosphere prevails everywhere until early morning when the crazies rest their heads for a few hours before starting all over again."

She refilled their coffee cups and sat beside Seth.

"The 'bad element' is thriving to such an extent that territorial disputes are endless. Seems like there's a murder every other week, one gangster or another is being gunned down."

Seth listened intently and then thanked Emmie for breakfast. He departed, intending to sight-see on the way to his destination. Although he had grown up near Chicago, just forty minutes away by train, Seth had visited the city only once when he was twelve.

As he walked, he remembered why the city held so much mystery and excitement: the Chicago Water Tower, the Fisher Building, the Marshall Field Building, the Navy pier, the Auditorium— each breathtaking. The roar of the trains overhead startled him at first. By contrast, the sing-song cries of the hucksters in the open markets had a lulling effect. The aromas associated with the river and the stockyards detracted from the aroma of food cooking, so many different smells, and sounds, and sights, that Seth had difficulty sorting them out. He hailed a cab and was soon standing in front of what appeared to be an oversized warehouse. As he pressed the front buzzer, he fumbled for a letter of recommendation from Blackie. A large man in shirtsleeves appeared.

"Who the hell are you?" he asked.

"Seth Shaw. I'm from New Orleans. Blackie sent me. I'm here to see Mr. Simboli at eleven. You may want to show him this."

Seth handed him the letter.

"Ah, you'll want to talk to Dominick. Stand there."

He pointed to a spot inside the doorway. In a few minutes, a young man appeared.

"So, you're the hotshot from New Orleans. Listen, we get riffraff coming here all the time looking for work. Unless you can shoot straight and fight well, we're not interested. From that bandage on your nose, it looks like someone had already put a brand on you."

"You should see the other guy," Seth said through clenched teeth.

No more than twenty-five years old, the young man was arrogant and self-assured beyond his years. Dark-skinned and handsome, he wasn't especially large, wearing blue suit pants, no coat, and showing a shoulder-holster over a wrinkled white shirt, no tie. His chiseled face was set off by a pencil mustache. His gleaming black hair smelled of tonic. His eyes were dark and piercing, a gold chain around his neck that disappeared inside his shirt collar, and he wore no wedding ring. Muscular and confident, he no doubt had his way with women.

"Can you shoot?" he asked.

"Of course."

"I'll let you prove it. We've got a range in a building out back."

When Seth put a tight pattern in the bullseye, Dominick's attitude changed abruptly.

"I'll take you to see my father now."

The pristine appearance of Carlos Simboli's office contrasted sharply with the disorderly setting inside the warehouse. The office easily accommodated an oversized glass-topped desk against one wall, two large sofas, and a conference table that could easily seat twelve people. When Carlos stood, Seth was struck by his neat appearance. He was almost a mirror image of his son—thin mustache, shiny black hair, blue suit, colorful tie, a dark-skinned Latino.

"So, you're the aspiring young man from Jazz Land," Carlos said, coming forward with hand extended. "I'm Carlos Simboli, and that poor specimen over there is my son, Dominick."

"Pleased to meet you both. I'm Seth Shaw."

Carlos sat in one of two leather chairs in front of his desk and gestured Seth to sit in the other. Dominick stood behind his father's chair.

"He's an excellent shot," Dominick said. "He trained in the Army sniper school during the war."

"Well, that could be helpful."

"We need a lot more than good shooting, though" Dominick said. "It's a question of character and guts. We don't hire just anybody. You may be a good shot, yes, but you're awfully young."

"I'm old enough," Seth said.

"Tell me about yourself," Carlos said.

Seth described everything, including the reason for his decision to leave Elgin, the trip to New Orleans, his position as bouncer in a brothel, his military stint, his connection to Blackie Condron, the assassination attempt, his broken nose, the double lynching.

"At your young age you've had some interesting things happen to you, more than most your age," Carlos said, glaring at his son. "Where did you first learn to shoot?"

"My stepfather taught me."

"You mentioned that you had criminal blood in your veins. How does that follow?"

"My biological father's name is Jefferson Smith better known as Soapy. He ran a criminal operation out of Skagway in the 1800's during the Klondike Gold Rush. And in some other cities to. He had a gang."

Seth gave details.

"Hold on! Hold on! You're telling me more than I need to know," Carlos said. He stood up to signal the end of the meeting. "You're hired."

Seth endured what Dominick called "a period of special training" for two weeks. At the end of that time, Carlos summoned him.

"I've got a special job for you. If you perform well, you'll continue to be one of us. If you fuck it up, we never heard of you. Got it?"

"Got it," Seth said.

"It will be a hit. Are you comfortable with that?"

"Yes."

"The man who will be your target has protection around him night and day, so you'll have to figure out how to get to him. It won't be easy."

"What do I need to know about him?"

"He's a boss in another part of town, an old man, but he refuses to step down. I've got every reason to believe that his two sons won't be greatly distressed if he's eliminated."

"That helps."

"After he's dead, his two boys might be inclined to do business with us. The old man has always shunned the idea. Do you think you could pull off something like that?"

"Just tell me where I can find him."

"His name is Roberto Gambini," Dominick said. "We'll provide details later. Right now, he's out of town visiting his daughter in Denver. Naturally, we'll take care of your expenses."

"I'll need some accessories."

"Like what?" Dominick asked.

"A good sniper rifle with a silencer, a scope, and a box of cartridges. I'll write down for you the brands I prefer."

"Dominick will arrange it."

"One other thing. The rifle has to be untraceable," Seth said.

"No problem," Dominick said. "We'll also give you a car that you can use while you're waiting."

Until his splint was removed, Seth remained in the boardinghouse except for one trip to the doctor and a few trips to the Chicago Library where he researched the Simboli and Gambini families.

Rising from nothing, Carlos Simboli ended up running the rackets for the entire North Side, and in the process becoming one of the strongest mob bosses in Chicago. He'd been the subject of several criminal investigations but had never been convicted. In his heyday, he was one of the best-dressed gangsters in town, and the handsomest. Although married, in the early years he is seen with one exotic woman on his arm after another. The stories describing Roberto Gambini, his rival, were similar except that he controlled the West Side. It is evident from the newspaper accounts that there had been friction between the two families for many years.

After Gambini returned from Denver, Dominick arranged a meeting with Seth at a nearby diner.

"The information you need is in this envelope," Dominick said, handing the item to Seth. "Memorize the information and then destroy the papers. By the way, we don't want the target wounded, we want him dead. And we'd like you to do it in the next two weeks, got it? By then, the splint on your nose should be history. Otherwise, you'll be a perfect target."

"Got it."

Christmas fast approached. Decorations were plentiful. To Seth it seemed like men dressed in Santa Claus suits were stationed on every corner. Despite the season, he told himself that he couldn't have doubts. After all, the target was a criminal who presumably had been involved in countless murders. Unfortunate as it was to be killing him during the holidays, it must be done. Seth's genetic imbalance was evidenced by the way he cavalierly embraced the ghastly assignment.

In his car, Seth followed Dominick to a parking lot behind what appeared to be an abandoned warehouse in need of repair. They entered through a crude cellar door and climbed dilapidated wooden stairs to the second floor. At the top of the stairs, with some difficulty, they pulled open one side of a set of metal doors and proceeded down a long hallway strewn with debris. A wooden door at the end opened to a room that was pitch-dark until Dominick turned on the light. They were standing in the main room of a tastily furnished apartment. The spotless interior had a blended decor. A couch and two easy chairs were upholstered with a handsome burgundy fabric. The drapes were dark blue. The pale gray carpet showed no evidence of dirt or wear. There was a bedroom and a kitchen further on.

"This is where you'll be confined until the job is done. The large living room window faces an alley at the end of which the Gambini offices are located."

Dominick pulled back the curtain and partially opened the shutter to point out the offices. Seth leaned in to have a look.

"From here you can observe old man Gambini when he comes and goes to and from his office. I'd advise you to keep this window shuttered and draped until the time comes. And if you're going to read at night, do it in the back bedroom with the bedroom door closed."

They moved into the back bedroom.

"The items you asked for are in the cello case in the corner."

"I can see that you've been planning this job for a long time. The apartment is proof of that," Seth said.

"It's how we keep tabs on our competition both visually and with the help of several bugs. When the system is operating it's like being in the same room."

Dominick continued. "You shouldn't go outside until the job is completed, but there's food in the refrigerator to last for several days. A lot is riding on you to carry this out without a hitch. When you give us the word, we'll position a truck beneath the kitchen window which overlooks a second alley in the back. The truck will have an enclosed bed filled with mattresses. When you've made the hit, simply jump out the window into the truck bed with the rifle in hand. Our driver will take it from there. As you pass the river, toss the rifle in after wiping it clean. It's untraceable, but we don't want fingerprints."

After Dominick left, Seth opened the cello case, delighted to discover a Mauser K98k, the sniper rifle he'd requested. Despite the five-round magazine and the silencer, Seth knew that he would be lucky to get off one round. Slowly he screwed the silencer into place using the threads located in the muzzle. Next, he inserted five rounds into the clip and put the clip in the chamber. Lastly, he adjusted the scope after opening the window shutter slightly to sight up the alley. Then he read the envelope of instructions. Before tearing up the papers and flushing them, Seth memorized the map giving the route to the safe house.

There was ample food in the refrigerator. As he ate a sandwich and drank a glass of milk, he wondered how to kill time until ready for bed. He found a pencil and blank paper in a kitchen drawer and began to write. The poems came easily after a few drafts.

DUST TO DUST
The strongest and the brightest
often feel that they
are on a higher plane
until death, the great equalizer,
turns all to dust.
Stable boys and kings
show the same amount of rust.

FOOTPRINT
Relentless in its pursuit
time blots out, erases, eliminates
the dirtiest marks
like rain in a muddy footprint.

The irony wasn't lost on him. There he was, an assassin coiled in his nest, waiting for the best time to strike, *and I'm writing poetry! Is anyone else suffering from the Black Dog so inspired?* Then he remembered crazy Vincent who left behind the greatest paintings the world has ever seen before committing suicide in a field in Flanders.

Seth began to study Gambini's schedule, discovering that he adhered to a fixed routine. At 9:30 a.m. exactly he would arrive each weekday morning in his limo, and at precisely 1:30 p.m. he emerged for lunch until 3 p.m. when he returned. At precisely 5:30 p.m., Gambini departed for the day, always in the same limo. His office was located on the first floor of a three-story brownstone showing a wide, stone stairway that led to the main entrance. It was one of several brownstones that lined the south side of Jackson Street, a quiet residential street in the city. In all cases, going or coming, the bodyguards gathered around Gambini.

Seth noted one peculiarity that occurred each morning. Just before Gambini climbed the stairs, invariably he stepped out of his protective bubble to buy a flower from a girl who was always in position at the foot of the stairs. He would then put the flower in his lapel and proceed upward. Seth concluded that this would be the perfect moment to make the hit, estimating no more than ten seconds to aim and fire. He told Dominick by phone that the hit would take place the following morning.

Waiting for the limo to arrive, Seth remained calm—no shaking hands, no wet palms, no measured breathing. Exactly on time, the black limousine arrived. As usual, the bodyguards formed a phalanx around Gambini that opened briefly to let him buy his flower. At that moment, Seth pulled the trigger. Spotting the red splotch on the victim's temple, Seth moved immediately to the back window and leaped out with rifle in hand. Fortunately, the truck was waiting in place. Later, when no one could observe, he threw the rifle into the river after wiping it to remove fingerprints.

Forty minutes later, Seth leaped over the side and gave the driver the high sign before walking to the spot where the designated car awaited with the keys under the front seat. He found the safe house with no difficulty after driving for a little over an hour. The farmhouse was stocked with provisions and books. Once again, Seth resorted to poetry to pass the time and ease his mind.

AFTER THE FALL
Adam is away gathering fruit.
Eve is at home in the backyard
reclining on a chaise.
Out of a hole in the ground
comes the serpent
that Eve hadn't seen
in many days.
"Eve, I wonder if you remember me?"

At first she froze,
but in short order
she once again became composed.
"How could I forget you?" she said.
"You prompted the disobedience
that caused all our woes."
The serpent responded:
"There are a few things you ought to know."
He paused to hiss, then went on.
"Most important, you were set up, my Dear.
It was part of God's plan to bring evil into the world.
The fallen angels that mankind came to fear
were part of it.
As you probably know, nothing falls
outside of God's ambit.
The same is true regarding
your reaction to the famous tree.
Have you ever seen how most children perform
when you place them unsupervised
in a room full of candy that is plentiful and free?
At the end of the day
no matter how much you exhort them,
most of the candy will be eaten away."
At first, Eve doesn't know what to say.
Then she pulled herself together
and answered in full voice.
"Are you telling me that God
treated me like a child knowing exactly
what I would do,
that I was a mere pawn?"
The snake shot back,
"Right on."
Remembering how beautiful Eden was,

Eve responded with a sheepish grin:
"Considering that the fall was a setup
is there any chance we can get back in?"

After thirteen days in hiding, Dominick appeared.

"Kid, you're a hero. My father thinks you're the greatest thing since Joan of Arc."

"I'll take your word for it. I haven't seen the papers."

"To say it went well would be an understatement. It was a clean hit, a perfect hit. His bodyguards didn't hear a thing, just watched him fold like a sack of rags. After a big funeral, Roberto's two sons, Jeano and Paulie, took over the operation. Soon they agreed to an alliance with us without raising any questions about the hit."

Dominic paused, then continued.

"I'm sure the Gambinis have figured out who was behind it. They found the apartment and destroyed it, but for whatever reason they've made no accusations. I got to be honest. I thought you'd fuck it up somehow, get yourself caught or miss your target or lose your nerve. You ended up impressing the family greatly, best of all, you've impressed my father."

"Thanks. Who took the blame?"

"The cops are reporting that it was an unknown assassin, probably someone from back East. They have no idea who did it. The whole thing went off without a hitch, which is a feather in your cap. My father wants you to become his personal bodyguard."

Caught off guard, Seth wondered whether the appointment would cause problems.

"I'm honored," he said, trying not to show reluctance. Flattered though he was, Seth felt intimidated. He had witnessed Carlos' anger, though never directed at him. And he would soon discover that Carlos could be downright affable, even witty in ways that Seth would never have imagined.

Although Carlos' craving for Italian food had in recent years given him a paunch, in Seth's view he still cut a fine figure, with a thin mustache and full head of hair and probably in his sixties. Seth had heard that if you make a friend of Carlos Simboli, you had a friend for life. On the other hand, if you cross him, you'd better start looking over your shoulder.

Seth and Dominick were riding in a car together after a long lunch.

"You must know that I'm very envious of you," Dominick said.

"How so?"

"I've been trying to get my father's respect for years, and I've failed miserably. Then you come along and win him over completely. You have his total respect."

"Come on, Dominick. You know he loves you."

"And he loves you just as much. The difference is that he respects you as well. He's never felt that way about me."

"Sure, he does. You know he's not one to express his emotions."

One month later, Seth received word that his mother and stepfather had burned to death in their Elgin home in a fire of suspicious origin. Even as estranged as the relationship with his parents had been, Seth's love for them had remained strong. He felt guilty that he hadn't been in touch since his departure, but he continued to be concerned that they would ask him about his work history—a bouncer in a whorehouse, hit man and bodyguard for gangsters. The minute he received the news, the Black Dog was upon him.

"Carlos, I've got to go to Elgin for a few days."

"Of course, you do. I just learned what happened. I'm very sorry."

"Thanks"

"Take all the time you need."

Seth grappled with the thought that Shorty and Libby might

have been murdered, most likely by a professional arsonist hired by a third party. First, he attended the joint memorial service. No other relatives were present. In fact, very few people were there at all. Seth watched both caskets being lowered into adjacent graves. Surprised at his emotions, he returned to the hotel and then spent the next three days talking to as many people as he could find about the tragedy—neighbors, fire officials, members of the police. He even poked around in the ashes of the burned-out structure. Finally, he met with Burley Jones, the reporter who had covered the incident. They had lunch together in a restaurant in downtown Elgin.

"Your stepfather was in the shipping business."

"That's correct, but he had several other businesses as well."

"Rumor has it that he entered into an arrangement with some local gangsters to ship illegal booze. After several months, he decided to get out. Unfortunately, because he knew too much, his gangster partners wouldn't let him do that. That's the theory at least."

"You mean they resorted to murder?"

"That's what my sources tell me, but I couldn't prove it one way or the other, and my boss at the paper wouldn't let me print the full story. I have one confirmation and need three. My suspicions, of course, are never printed."

"You're saying that these creatures murdered Libby during an attack on Shorty?"

"That's about it."

"Do you know who is responsible?"

"At this point I can only speculate, but I've got a pretty good idea."

"Tell me."

"Two brothers recently come into control of an underworld empire after their father was assassinated."

"Say no more. I know who they are."

"You do?"

"Yes, Jeano and Paulie Gambini," Seth said

"That's correct. How is it that you know their names?" Jones asked.

"Just a good guess. Mind you, I'm not saying they did it themselves."

"Save your breath. I know how these cowards operate. They get some low life to do the dirty work for them," Jones said

"Correct."

Seth didn't tell Jones that he himself qualified or that his boss, Carlos Simboli, ordered the hit.

"There's an attorney you should talk to," Jones said. "I think he has information you can use. I'm pretty sure he's handling the estate."

The reporter thought for a moment.

"His name is Negley, Duane Negley. He has an office nearby. Don't be fooled by the way he looks. His scruffy appearance belies his underlying brilliance. I don't think he's ever lost a case."

Seth went immediately to Negley's office, which was as disheveled as its occupant appeared to be—papers strewn everywhere, books of all types jammed into two tottering bookshelves with bookmarks in place, file folders piled high on the desk, cock-eyed Venetian blinds. Negley appeared to be in his mid-fifties with hair greying at the temples, a spreading bald spot, wrinkled face, and stained suit. Thin and short, Negley's long neck gave him the look of some sort of exotic bird. If Jones hadn't touted the man's brilliance, Seth would have walked away.

They sat together at a small conference table.

"Mr. Shaw, I've been trying to find you for some time. You're in line to inherit a substantial sum of money. To make funds available for you upon her death, your mother opened a trust fund for your benefit to which your stepfather also contributed. It has been in place for a long time and has grown apace."

"First things first," Seth huffs. "What can you tell me about their demise? Was it really a planned hit?"

"I'm afraid so. The circumstances point in that direction. However, there isn't enough direct evidence to pin anybody. I'm pressuring the district attorney to investigate further."

"Why were they killed?"

"A rumor is spreading that an unsavory element wanted to put Shorty down. Supposedly, your father knew too much about certain illegal operations."

"Why would he get tied in with these people? He had the necessary assets and acumen to make money the honest way."

"A short time before his death, Shorty came to see me. To him Prohibition was a joke. Law enforcement is totally ineffective, and most officers are on the take. The law simply looks the other way. On top of that, your stepdad thought he could keep the illegal part separate from his regular business operations, after all, he was nothing more than a middleman.

"I advised him not to do it, but he didn't listen."

"How long did he stay in?"

"Two years, long enough to make a killing, and long enough to see his mistake. That's when he came to see me," Negley said.

"The criminal element wasn't about to let him walk?" Seth added.

"Correct. It had been a perfect connection for the Gambinis. They relied on your stepfather's fleet of vessels without having to make any capital investment of their own, an ideal setup."

"Too ideal."

"When he told them he wanted out, they told him to reconsider. He refused. Then Shorty threatened go to the authorities if they didn't stop hounding him. I warned him about making threats. Once again, he didn't listen. I expect that's when they decided to take him out."

"The bastards! Since it's obvious who is behind it, why can't we nab them?"

"No direct proof. The evidence is all circumstantial."

"What about tracking down the arsonist or arsonists?"

"Same problem. No evidence. No trail. Probably from out of town. I'm so sorry. My wife and I considered Shorty and Libby to be close personal friends. As a matter of fact, they often spoke of you, always in glowing terms."

Seth sat silently as Negley reached for the topmost file on his desk.

"You must let me tell you about your inheritance."

Negley described the estate, which amounted to approximately thirty million dollars, and a separate trust with another five million. He explained that he planned to liquidate the assets as soon as possible now that Seth had been located, with the caveat that some assets, such as real estate and maritime equipment, might take some time to dispose of. He added that the insurance settlement on the death claims arrived only recently.

"Wow, that's a lot of money. What bank holds the trust?" Seth asked.

"Elgin Bank and Trust."

"Is that the bank owned by the Davidson family?"

"Yes."

"How much time will you need to convert everything into cash?"

"A few months except for the assets I mentioned," Negley said.

Seth asked for details about the trust at the bank.

"The good news is that the trust assets, mostly marketable securities, can be converted into cash quite readily."

"If the assets in the trust are converted into cash, is there anything to prevent me from closing the trust and withdrawing the funds?"

"You can close the trust and withdraw funds when you turn twenty-one, which I expect occurred some years ago. That being the case, there is nothing to prevent you from closing it now, although you can expect the bank to squawk if you decide to do so."

"Who's head of the bank at this point?"

"A young man by the name of Lowery Davidson, the grandson of the founder. Do you know him?"

"I've had the pleasure," Seth smirked. "Mr. Negley, you've done a great job on all this, a fantastic job. I'd like you to represent me personally if that's agreeable."

"Perfectly. I'll have my secretary bring in a client letter."

When she arrived with the letter, Seth signed it on the spot.

"Can you keep a confidence?" Seth asked.

"Of course, you now receive the benefit of what is known as the attorney-client privilege. Everything we discuss from this point forward remains confidential."

"When you brought up Lowery Davidson's name, you probably noticed an inadvertent reaction on my part. Let me tell you why."

For several minutes Seth gave details regarding the unfortunate incident in Elgin beginning with a description of his relationship with Connie Davidson. He described in detail the incident in front of the Davidson residence, the false accusation of theft, the planned expulsion from Elgin Academy, the decision to move south, and the resulting life of crime.

"If you didn't feel a deep-seated bitterness toward the Davidson family, you'd be a saint," Negley said.

"Given the bad blood between our families, why did my parents keep their money in the Davidons' bank."

"I can't say for certain, Seth, but it was probably a way for your stepfather to keep the peace with the Davidsons. As you know, they are a power family."

"Makes sense," Seth paused. "Here's what I want you to do. Give Davidson all the financials relating to the estate. He already knows about the trust. Once he calculates how much money would be involved, tell him that I most likely would keep the current trust in place. Tell him also that I plan to pour the proceeds from the estate assets into the trust."

"But you don't really intend to do that, do you?" Negley asked.

"No, I don't. But I want you to be convincing. Also, I'd like you to set up a meeting with Davidson at the bank."

"Got it."

CHAPTER ELEVEN

H aving completed his investigation in Elgin, Seth returned
to Chicago to attend a dinner at Rivoli's Restaurant, Carlos'
favorite spot. Seth entered, moving past photo displays
of celebrities and friends hanging along the hallway walls leading
to the dining room—Frank Sinatra, Tony Bennett, Sammy Davis
Junior, Dean Martin, and other prominent figures all smiling at the
camera in signed photos. Once through the hallway, Seth paused in
the doorway into the dining room to take stock of the layout. On
the walls of the expansive eating area were several paintings, all bad
ones, of Italian landscapes, oil on black velvet.

Toward the front was a single circular table covered by a red-
checkered tablecloth around which sat several members of the
Simboli crime family. The rest of the place was empty. Carlos had
followed his customary practice of taking over the entire restaurant
for the evening. Carlos had removed his suitcoat revealing a shoulder
holster hanging under his left arm. His white shirt was immaculate,
with starched cuffs and gold cuff links. Dominick sat to his left,
a carbon copy of his father except that Dominick's white shirt
was wrinkled and dirty, particularly at the cuffs. Seth noted that
Dominick's shoulder holster and coat were hanging behind his chair.

Next to Dominick sat Horace Guttman, the trusted consigliore,
with grey suitcoat removed, and no weapon in evidence. Both a
lawyer and CPA, Guttman specialized in money laundering and tax

evasion. His white shirt, opened at the collar, exposed matted hair. Next to Guttman sat Rico Contesta, another bodyguard who was some fifteen years older than Seth. His holster cradled a Smith & Wesson revolver. Rico was infamous for his quick temper. Seth noted of the empty chair beside Carlos.

Carlos shouted a welcome to Seth and pointed to the empty chair. Seth had hoped for a private meeting; he wanted to tell Carlos that he'd be leaving the family. Seth knew Carlos wouldn't be happy with the news. The two men had developed a deep and trusting friendship.

Seth scanned the layout of the room and was uneasy. There was a hallway on the left that led to an outside door past the restrooms, and a hallway on the right that led past the photo gallery and another outside door. There was a third door to the outside through the kitchen. A potential gunman would have several avenues of attack, and the family would be sitting ducks. Seth had expressed his reservations about Rivoli's in the past, but to no avail.

The management and staff of Rivoli's had pulled out all the stops. Three bottles of Chianti were in place on the large circular table alongside three baskets of Italian bread and three large bowls of spaghetti. Seth was about to serve himself when a voice in his head said that he should immediately drop to the floor and move under the table for cover, which he did only seconds before a gunman appeared. The other diners remained frozen in their seats with no time to reach for weapons or to run for their lives. From the far side of the room a stuttering fusillade of bullets erupted from a single tommy gun creating an ear-shattering crescendo. The sound of bullets ripping into flesh continued for several seconds. Attempting to stand, Carlos was knocked backward by the force of four rounds in his chest causing him to rebound off the back wall and fall forward under the table. Carlos, with blood gushing from various wounds, fell on top of Seth.

The single shooter departed in a matter of seconds, charging out the front door and into an awaiting car. Seth was unhurt but chose not to move until he was certain the gunman had departed. Still lying prone, he checked Carlos' wrist for a pulse and found none. As he lay dying, Carlos' blood soaked Seth.

Certain that the gunman was gone, Seth rose to scan the carnage. The room was a shambles, chairs overturned, spaghetti blasted into grotesque shapes on the floor and walls, wine and blood spattered everywhere. Somehow the round oak table, thick and heavy, remained standing, although riddled with ugly pock marks on the surface where bullets had struck. Targeted members of the dinner party lay blood-soaked and unmoving on the white-and-black tile floor. The acrid smell of gunpowder permeated the air.

The salvo had been deafening. When Seth's ears stopped ringing, he heard the screams coming from various victims. One waiter shot in the side bellowed in severe pain. The kitchen staff, all women, were sobbing and screaming. Seth headed quickly for the back door. Once outside, he noted his blood-soaked clothing. The shooter obviously assumed that he was dead or had failed to notice him in the smoke and excitement. Seth feared that the assassin and his accomplices would come looking for him once the newspapers provided a body count. His apartment would be the first place they would look so he couldn't go there. The police weren't an option either because so many of them were corrupt.

When Seth heard distant sirens, he fled, not really knowing where to go. Wandering for some time, he came upon a Catholic church, Saint Alphonsus, located on West Wellington Avenue. Out front, he removed his shoulder holster and gun. The leather was caked with blood, so he tried unsuccessfully to wipe it clean with his shirt cuff before hiding the items behind a bush. Finding the main door open, he walked through.

"Excuse me, Father."

"My heavens, what's happened to you?" the priest said.

"Can I talk to you in private?" Seth asked.

"Go to the confessional—over there." He pointed with the large Bible that he was holding.

The priest was a young man, tall and stocky, probably in his late twenties with thick, black, wavy hair and fair skin. His white collar contrasted sharply with his black shirt, dark trousers, and black shoes. Once inside the confessional, Seth noticed a small window in the wall in front of him.

"Are you Catholic?" the voice asked.

"No, Father, I'm not sure what I am."

"Are you hurt?"

"No, not a scratch on me, a miracle, plain and simple. An assassin tried to kill me and several others."

"We can get into the details later. For the time being just tell me what you think the church can do for you."

Seth explained that he needed a place to hide out until things quieted down a bit, insisting that he'd be gone in a few days and needed only a few days, adding that if the church turned him over to the police or forced him out, *you'll be signing my death warrant.* Seth advised that the identity of the gunman was unknown.

The voice on the other side of the screen was soft and soothing, which encouraged Seth to think that the man might be willing to help out of kindness. The priest's next suggestion was that they move from the confessional to his personal office. *Thankfully, there's been no move to bring in the police,* Seth thought.

Inside the priest's office were wall shelves packed with books flanking a small desk and two leather chairs. The priest sat in one and motioned Seth to the other.

"By the way, my full name is John Conti, but everyone calls me Father John."

"I thank you for your kindness, Father John. Please call me Seth."

He gave a brief description of the events at Rivoli's, acknowledging that he was saved by a miracle, though he was at a loss to explain why God would favor him when his faith had always been lukewarm. His mother and stepfather believed, he said, but the time restraints presented by his stepfather's many business operations impeded any sort of regular attendance. His stepfather often discussed religious topics during hunting excursions on Saturdays, but a chance for conversation on any other day during the remainder of the week had been rare.

Seth described his forced departure from Elgin, admitting to his uncontrollable temper and the brutal consequences that come from it. He told of his tribulations in New Orleans and how he fell in with the Chicago mob. The source of the bad choices, he said, came from the bad blood inherited from his biological father. He described Soapy's criminal tendencies.

"The Devil made you do it. Is that it? I've heard that argument before," Father John said.

"But you don't buy that argument, do you?" Seth said.

"I need to hear more. Did you ever contact your parents after you left Elgin?" he asked.

"No. I couldn't bring myself to do that."

"Why?"

"They would have asked questions about my job choices, and I couldn't lie to them."

Seth gave details.

"I see your point," Father John said.

As further background, Seth explained that his stepfather was deeply in love with Libby almost from their first meeting and had no hesitancy about marrying her even while pregnant with another man's child.

"Unfortunately, Libby was an unintended victim who died in the same housefire set by a hired arsonist who set out to eliminate Shorty," Seth said.

Seth assured Father John that his stepfather was an honest man who made one glaring mistake and suffered for it.

"Tell me more about Soapy Smith."

Seth continued without embellishments. He spoke of Soapy's rebellion against respectability even when his siblings were successful pillars of their communities—lawyers, bankers, judges, and important political figures. He described Soapy's role in Skagway as the criminal mastermind, the evil operations that came forth, and the fury that emerged when Soapy was crossed.

"From what you're telling me, it sounds like Soapy was suffering from bipolar disease," Father John said.

"You should know that my friend Keano, before his death, described a condition that affected his father and brother the same way. They called it the Black Dog."

"Same thing. Black Dog is another name for bipolar illness—tragic spells of depression combined with overriding mania. It's also known as bipolar disorder and as manic-depressive illness," Father John said.

"Bingo!" Seth said.

"And here's the most important part of it, the disease has a genetic component," Father John said.

"Which means?"

"It can be passed on from one generation to another," Father John said.

"Double Bingo! That means I'm not out in left field when I talk about an aberration in the blood affecting me."

"And the most important part of it, in your case, is that the bipolar illness you are suffering is tied to Soapy Smith," Father John said.

"How does it happen that you know so much about such things?" Seth asked.

"My major in college was psychology. I went on to get a master's degree and a doctorate before taking my vows. I was a late bloomer," Father John laughed.

"But there is something else. The final irony is that my parents escaped the Great Fire and Earthquake in San Francisco only to burn to death in a fire set by an arsonist."

"A tragic turn of events. I'm so sorry," Father John said.

"Such tragedies keep happening, one after the other. These

horrific events in my life are so horrendous and so frequent that in my view they cannot be regarded as chance happenings. I'm sure they devolve from a separate curse," Seth said.

"Now you're reaching a bit," Father John said.

The priest went silent for a few minutes. Then, he said what Seth had been hoping to hear. "Even if I were to find you quarters here in the church, you couldn't stay long."

"Three days is all I'll need, Father," Seth said.

"You may have done ugly things, but you have a good face and I sense you have a good soul underneath. For that reason, I'm going to take a chance on you."

Seth followed him to the room in the rectory, sparsely furnished with dark, ponderous furniture, old and worn, a single bed set to one side, a desk, two end tables, a high chest, three straight-back chairs, an armoire and three huge bookcases. A long table in the middle of the room was covered with papers and open books. A large Bible with a bookmark sat on one of the end tables. A crucifix above the bed was the only object aside from two casement windows set in the four grey walls.

"You 'll be safe here. No one will bother you."

Father John left and returned with fresh towels and a change of clothes.

"The best thing you can do right now," he said, "Is to get some sleep after you've cleaned up a bit. You've had quite an ordeal. The bathroom and shower are up the hall."

After a quick shower, Seth crawled into bed and was asleep in minutes. Father John arrived in the morning carrying a tray of hot food.

"This won't happen often," he said, smiling as he handed over the tray. "You slept very well. It's close to one thirty in the afternoon.

Even so, I'm able to get a breakfast for you."

"Thank you."

The wonderful aroma of eggs, toast and bacon filled the room. Having slept for so long, Seth was famished.

"I've got the morning paper for you," the priest said, handing it to Seth. "I'm not sure you'll want to see it. Your fateful dinner party is described in detail."

"You bet I want to see it."

Seth spread the paper on the tray. The front page called the incident a "gangland shooting." Four diners had been killed by an unknown gunman, and a fifth diner had escaped. The four victims were described as members of the well-known and notorious Simboli gang.

"How can you be part of it?" Father John asked.

"It isn't easy, Father. It takes a real son-of-a-bitch, a killer like me, to make the connection, but hopefully that's behind me now."

"You should be grateful you're alive."

"I can attest to that. The last thing I remember is diving for the floor after a voice in my head told me to take cover, seconds before the gunman arrived. If Carlos' body hadn't fallen on top of me, I'd most likely be dead. There's no reason for God to spare me, but He did."

"What do you plan to do about that?" Father John asked.

"Father, I'd like to shed the old skin and become a new man."

"Do you really mean that?"

"Yes, I do."

The priest rose to leave the room, making a pronouncement. "I can see that you're sincere. I can help you make your spiritual connection."

By the time the priest returned, Seth had showered, dressed, and made the bed. He was sitting in one of the chairs reading the paper.

"You mentioned that you planned to shed your skin, which I take to mean that you want to be born again."

"That's it."

"Do you have any idea what it takes to accomplish that?"

"None at all. Am I too far gone, Father?"

"Not at all. You need only to ask Jesus Christ to come into your heart and mean it."

"And that's it?"

"That's it."

Seth changed the subject.

"On the train out here, I was annoyed by a fellow passenger. I now see now that what he told me about NDEs, and DIs was not just hype," Seth said.

"NDEs?"

"Yes, near death experiences, people who are stone dead who come back to tell us about what they observe. In most cases they describe a soothing, all-encompassing light that turns out to be Jesus Christ himself. They describe Heaven in glowing terms and tell of their conversations with the Almighty," Seth said.

"DIs?"

"Divine interventions."

Seth explained what they were. Father John had questions.

"Back to the NDEs as you call them. How can a person survive if all bodily functions are shut down?"

"Exactly. I posed the same question to the stranger. Since then, I think I've figured it out. It's the soul, Father. The soul is what remains alive to carry us forward after death and let us return. The voice that came to me, the one that saved me, comes from the same place. It's real, Father. It's all real."

Seth wiped his tears and excused himself.

While Seth used the bathroom, Father John took the tray back to the kitchen and threw Seth's bloody clothes into the trash bin. He then returned to Seth's room.

"What if this new commitment to Christ is just a whim, a temporary phase you're going through?" Father John asked.

"It's not just a phase or a whim, Father, believe me. This is the real thing. I saw my life flash before me as I'm lying bloody on that floor, and it wasn't a pretty picture."

Father John changed the subject.

"I'm not the only priest in attendance at Saint Alphonse. Father Reardon is the chief pastor. You'll have to get final approval to stay from him. He is away on retreat at present but returns tomorrow. I'll fill him in, but I'm sure he'll want to talk to you personally. Meanwhile, I'll advise the staff. There'll be no problems on that end."

"You're very kind."

The next day, Seth knocked on the door to Father Reardon's office.

"Come in," a gruff voice answered. Seth was immediately struck by the office's huge size. Father Reardon, dressed in black with a priest's collar, remained seated as Seth entered. He was a large man in his sixties with grey hair, a bulbous nose and skin pock-marked and red.

"Mr. Shaw, I'm not happy with what's going on here. I've seen the newspapers. You're part of the worst element of society. My colleague has made a huge mistake in offering you sanctuary. If the bishop finds out we're harboring a criminal, it won't go well for any of us."

"I understand completely, Father. I'll be gone in three days. I promise."

"Well, see that you are. And don't expect me to be tolerant if you're here one minute past the deadline."

"Agreed."

"You're excused."

Seth quickly walked up the hall to Father John's office where after knocking he found the priest at work at his desk.

"How'd things go with Papa?"

"Papa's not at all happy."

"Go on."

"Let's just say he won't be pleased if I remain beyond the deadline."

"Three days?"

"Three days."

"Father, has this ever happened before?"

"Has what ever happened?"

"Has someone as evil as I am ever offered to accept Christ?"

"Why, I can think of a perfect example. The Bible tells us of Paul, but he was worse, much worse, than you are."

Father John abruptly stood. "Before his transformation, Paul is involved in persecuting Christians. Using the name Saul, he is responsible for the death and torture of many. Then, on the road to Damascus he observes a light from above suddenly flash before him. When he falls to his knees, he hears a voice say to him, 'Saul, Saul why do you persecute me?' Whereupon Saul asks, 'who are you, Lord?' prompting the Lord to answer, 'I am Jesus, whom you are persecuting. Now get up and go into the city, and you will be told what to do.'"

"Wow! That's what I call a real conversion," Seth said.

"Yes, and when Saul stands up, he finds that he cannot see because his eyes are covered with scales. That condition is later cured by Ananias, the man Saul is told to contact. After three days, Ananias at the direction of the Lord lays hands on Saul and cures him in a way that makes the scales over his eyes drop away. Soon after that, Saul becomes known as Paul, an ardent advocate for the Lord."

"Father, when I talk about my own conversion, I may be reaching a bit. Certainly, there is no temporary blindness. Yes, I escaped from a point-blank fusillade at the restaurant, and I did hear a voice in my head, but it was probably my imagination. What if the hit man was a lousy shot?"

"Nonsense! You can't think that way. The odds of his missing you are a million to one. The hit man had no trouble killing the other four."

"God's a busy person," Seth said. "Aren't we pushing things a bit to think that he'll spend time messing with the likes of me?"

"All of us are special in God's eyes." Father John paused. "What are you doing for lunch?"

"Is it that time already? I'm open for any place except Rivoli's."

They both laughed.

"It's too dangerous for you to go out. We'll eat in our kitchen."

In the kitchen Ava, the cook, offered sandwiches and soup. The men took their places at a long wooden table.

CHAPTER TWELVE

T

wo days into Seth's stay at St. Alphonsus, Father John summoned him to the library.

"I recently got a message from my brother Robert who is on the police force. He tells me that a police officer on his beat found your shoulder holster and gun. Since it's discovered covered with blood on it outside this church, it won't take a genius to figure out where the blood came from, and where that person might be hiding. It's just a matter of time before the police come looking for you. We've got to get you out of here right now."

"I have two important questions," Seth said. "First, how am I going to get out of here without being seen, and second, where will I go when I do get out—assuming I can pull off the first miracle?"

"Leave all that to me and my family. My brother Charles, an undertaker, will be arriving in about an hour in a hearse carrying a single empty casket," Father John said.

"And I'm to be hauled out of here in that?"

"Correct."

"How will you manage that? I'm a very heavy specimen."

"Well, we've got the church maintenance crew to help, plus my brother and I."

"That should be enough. And what happens after that?"

"My sister Rosanne has a boardinghouse in the inner city. You'll be safe there."

Seth laughed. "Just how large is your family, anyway?"

"Large enough—three sisters and three brothers."

"I owe you and your family a lot."

"That's what we're here for, now let's get moving. Charles will be arriving soon."

It wasn't an experience that Seth would elect to repeat—confined space, blackness, muffled voices.

"Welcome to the land of the living," Charles said, as he removed the lid, finally.

"Don't ask me to do that again," Seth said, laughing.

"Look at it this way. The next time you do it, you won't feel a thing," Charles laughed.

Charles was a youthful and vigorous middle-ager, a big man Seth's size with ham hands and a walrus mustache, a ruddy complexion with bright brown eyes and a booming voice. When he laughed, his entire body shook causing his thin black hair to fall over his forehead.

"As you may have guessed, I'm Charles," he said.

"Pleased to meet you, Charles."

"My brother has told me all about you."

"Where am I?"

"You're in the basement of my sister's boardinghouse located in downtown Chicago. I'm one of her borders, and I suspect that you'll soon be one as well."

"How many borders are there?"

"Six. It's not quite a full house."

"How do I know we can trust them all? If word gets out that I'm here, I'm dead meat."

"The borders are all good boys. I know each one personally. In fact, one of them is my sister's fiancé. No one is going to snitch."

"I'll take your word for that."

"Come on upstairs. I'll introduce you."

They came upon Rosanne in the hallway. Immediately, Seth was struck by her lissome figure as she stood in front of an open doorway with the sun's rays silhouetting her body. As she moved forward to extend her hand, Seth noticed faint specks of perspiration on her forehead beside a loose strand of dark hair, delicate evidence of the menial task she had been undertaking seconds earlier. Though disheveled and embarrassed about being caught in a plain skirt and apron, her beauty was undiminished. Seth glared at her dark grey eyes, long lashes, and swanlike neck. *It's just my luck she's been promised to another.*

"I'd like to stay and talk, but I've got chores to do," Rosanne said. "Charles will show you to your room."

Later, at dinner, Seth was introduced to the borders—Garth and Peter, followed by Vincent, Cody, and Mathew.

Except for Charles, all the men worked the docks as stevedores.

"It's kind of a tradition. If you work the docks, you board at Rosie's," said Peter, a young man in his twenties.

"By now, you probably know that Rosie is the woman of my dreams," Cody said. "She recently consented to be my bride, after a year of begging on my part, making me a very lucky man."

"You've got yourself a real beauty there," Matt said.

"And remember, Cody, just in case you decide to make a move on her before the wedding, she is my sister."

Everyone laughed as Charles pounded his fist into his palm.

The boardinghouse was exceptionally clean. The hardwood floors sparkled, and the long table used for meals had been cleaned and polished with place settings already in place. When the food arrived, it was obvious to Seth after one or two bites that Rosie was as good a cook as she was a housekeeper. That day she served roast chicken, mashed potatoes with gravy and green beans. Little was said as the meal progressed until a question was directed at Seth.

"Just what do you do?" Peter asked.

"Now is a good time as any for me to interrupt," Charles said. "I knew that question would come up sooner or later. Please bring Rosie out of the kitchen. She ought to hear this, too."

He waited for Rosie to appear then related Seth's story in graphic detail.

"You mean he's on the lam?" Peter asked.

"Exactly, and I've told him that he can trust all of us to keep our mouths shut," Charles said. "It truly is a matter of life and death."

"Our lips are sealed," Peter said. "There are no canaries here."

"That's good, because Seth's life depends on it."

Seth interjected. "I want to tell everybody that I've done some rotten things. Since the attack at Rivoli's, though, I've decided to shed my old skin if that's possible. I should be dead, but I'm alive. I'm not sure why, but that's the way of it."

"You've decided to accept Christ," Peter said.

"Yes."

With this last comment, Seth glared into Rosie's eyes and felt his heart begin to pound.

"How long do you expect to be here?" Matt asked.

"Father John thinks it should be two months, at least," Charles said. "It'll take that long for things to die down. Obviously, Seth will have to stay indoors. In the meantime, Father John assures me that the church will cover all expenses including the cost of his room."

Time passed. Bored at being confined, Seth welcomed word from Charles that Father John would be stopping by. When he arrived, Seth was waiting in the parlor.

"Father John, there's something I need to ask you," Seth said a few minutes into the conversation.

"Oh?"

"It's pretty clear that the Gambinis had my parents killed."

"And you're wondering whether vengeance would be justified?"

"Yes."

"'Vengeance is mine sayeth the Lord.' Just remember that bit of scripture any time you feel tempted to take things into your own hands."

"There's something else," Seth said.

"Fire away."

"Despite my best efforts to fight it, I find myself very attracted to your sister."

"Whoops, you're aware that Rosie's been spoken for?"

"I am."

"What do you propose to do about that?"

"Nothing, absolutely nothing. I don't intend to say a word, but I wanted you to know."

Fate had other plans. Just a week later Cody was killed in a freak accident at the docks. He was working beneath a crane when a load slipped. All of Rosie's boarders—Garth, Peter, Vincent, Mathew, Charles, and Seth—were gathered at Charles' funeral home.

"Rosie is taking it badly," Charles said. "And so am I. The guy was almost my brother-in-law. I loved him as much as she did. A good man, a caring person."

"He was only twenty-nine years old," Matt said. "Too young to die."

The memorial service entailed a brief eulogy, nothing more. All the boarders at Rosie's were pall bearers including Seth. Following the final prayer by Father John at the grave site, Charles pulled Seth aside.

"Cody has a premonition that something awful was going to happen to him. He worried that he might be dead before the marriage. He told me to talk to you if something happened."

"To me?"

"Yes, Seth, to you. Cody was a very compassionate man and very observant. He noticed the way you and Rosie looked at each other and was convinced that you both felt a deep attraction."

"He detected that?"

"Yes. And Cody was also appreciative that you never pursued that attraction, that you were respectful of his engagement to her."

Charles began to walk slowly away from the graveside as Seth followed.

"You can imagine how difficult it was for Cody, to tell me this. Still, he did so out of concern for Rosie."

"I understand."

"Let me cut to the chase. He wanted you to know that it would be okay for you to be with Rosie."

"What a fantastic guy," Seth said.

Alone in his room later that day Seth returned to his poetry.

TIME DOESN'T LEAVE US ALONE
Time doesn't leave us alone.
Today's baby girl
becomes tomorrow's toothless crone
and our beloved four-star general
with a hero's crust
becomes in time
a solitary gravestone
over a pile of dust.

A COACH AND FOUR
I watch as a coach and four
clatters through the open gate
into a cobble-stoned courtyard
with speed set at the highest rate
scattering chickens and dogs
along the way
before halting in a cloud of tumult
at the Inn's oversized front door.

One man in livery
climbs down from the rear
to throw open the coach door
while a second calms the steaming horses,

both servants pleased
to be part of the metaphor.

Craning heads
from the windows above
watch as a large man emerges
obviously, a bit of a prig
with lace at the collar,
frock coat shining,
and adorned in silk stockings
that match his white wig.

Make way for the King,
is the shouted command
of the page holding the horse's bit,
and right away I become aware
that I'm trapped inside the dream
of some unsuspecting Brit.

In the midst of his sorrow and bliss, Seth struggled to muzzle the
Black Dog. His frustration about his confinement had summoned
dark feelings. He had hoped Rosie would pull him into the light. In
the morning he asked her to join him in the library.

"I'm getting cabin fever," Seth said.

"That may be, but you're supposed to remain in hiding."

"It's been long enough. Will you please go somewhere with me?
No one will see us, I promise. As I sit here rotting, the world is taking
on a new shape. Crazy things are happening in Europe."

"You've got it all figured out, haven't you?"

"I'll tell you something else. The *peace* that came after the Great
War was no peace at all. It was an intermission."

Seth began pacing.

"You do have the jim-jams, don't you?" she said.

"The jim-jams?"

"Yes, the nervous twitches."

"You're damn right I do. I've got to get out of here, even if it's only for a few hours, even if it's only for a cup of coffee."

Rosie acquiesced. They went for coffee, then to a museum. Next, they spent hours in the public library and finally, the movies. Inevitably, the affection between them turned into love. He found her in the kitchen preparing breakfast.

"Rosie, you must know by now how I feel about you. I'm madly in love with you, so much so, in fact, that I won't be happy on this earth until you agree to marry me."

She smiled. "Seth Shaw, is that a proposal?"

"You're damn right it is."

"Well, then . . . I accept."

He grabbed her and kissed her, lifting her off the ground while making a sound very much like an Indian war whoop.

"I have a huge inheritance waiting for me in Elgin, Illinois. It will become *our* fortune once we're married. If anything happens to me, I want you to contact Attorney Duane Negley in Elgin. He's a good man, totally trustworthy and knows the full story."

"Duane Negley," she repeated.

"You'd never know it to look at him but he's a brilliant lawyer."

"How much money are we talking about?" she asked.

"About thirty-five million before taxes and fees, plus a trust fund at Elgin Bank with an additional five million."

"*Holy Christopher!* No wonder I fell in love with you."

The wedding ceremony occurred before a justice of the peace in Elgin. Charles and the others were present as was Father John, who officiated. Later, in Duane Negley's office, Seth received a check representing the sale price of the estate assets. Next, they executed the wills that Negley had prepared, and then left for a meeting with Davidson.

The bank building was impressive, with high marble columns, frescoed ceilings, crystal chandeliers and multiple teller windows that appeared to be embarrassingly unbusy. Seth, Rosie and Negley were sitting in deep leather chairs around an impressive mahogany table in the bank's main conference room. Abruptly, Lowery Davidson entered through a door at the far end of the room. His moustache was gone; his long blond hair receded into balding patches. As he spoke, neck flaps waggled. Seth tempered his critical observations when recalling that Lowery wasn't that much older than he.

Davidson began the conversation following the necessary introductions.

"I understand from Duane that you want to close out the trust. I'm prepared to give you a check in the full amount," Davidson said.

Seth pounded his fist on the table.

"That's all you've got to say after your family ruined my life, that *you're prepared to give me a check!* That's it?"

"Stay calm, Seth. You don't want to do anything rash," Rosie said.

"Do you remember me at all? Are you aware of what your family did to me?"

"Yes, I remember you, and I'm sorry it happened. It was my father's idea, but you should also remember that you gave me a pretty good licking."

"Fact is you deserved the licking."

"Yes, I did."

"And your father took it from there."

"I'm truly sorry for that."

"I'm not buying any of it," Seth said.

"Hold on, Seth. He seems to be sincere," Rosie said.

Davidson continued. "One way to look at this is to say that anyone who has a fortune as large as yours is doing pretty well despite past difficulties."

"The fortune, however large, doesn't begin to pay for the pain I've encountered."

"There is one thing I can offer that may help a little," Davidson said.

"What are you talking about?"

"Simple. I know the people who want to kill you, and I can call them off."

"What? How can you do that?"

"Where do you think most members of the criminal element in Chicago keep their money? Not in the city where the feds or rival gangs can grab it. No, they choose small, safe banks like this one. Over the years, I've met a lot of interesting characters."

"Like Jeano and Paulie Gambini?"

"Yes . . . and many others."

"It's all beginning to come clear," Seth said.

"Considering the size of the assets in your trust, they suspected that you'd be coming to see me sooner or later," Davidson said.

"Tell me more."

"Under one scenario, the Gambinis send someone to track you down and kill you. Under another, they work with you to make a deal."

"What kind of a deal?"

"As the Gambinis see it, the scales are evenly balanced. You killed their father. They killed your boss."

"And three other members of the Simboli crime family, and don't forget my mother and stepfather, who were burned to death in a suspicious fire. I don't need balance."

"Seth, listen to him," Rosie said.

"Keep talking," Seth said.

"Here's the deal. If you agree to deposit the assets from the estate sale in the trust, and leave the trust here at the bank, they'll call off the dogs."

"Why would they do that?"

"The funds will strengthen the bank. That will benefit them. My family owns it in name only."

"What happens if I don't agree?"

"I'll have to tell them where to find you. You can imagine what will happen after that."

"Can you give us some privacy? I need to talk this over with my wife and my attorney."

Davidson left the conference room.

"Duane, I don't trust the son-of-a-bitch. What do you think?" Seth asked.

"I don't see that you have much choice, unless you want to end up dead."

"Why are they interested in my money? Do they intend to steal it?"

"I think not. I think your money will be safe, but the total will help fortify the bank's balance sheet. That's agreeable to them, and there's no other way you can call them off. You've got to go along."

"I agree," Rosie said.

After a brief discussion Seth called Davidson back in.

"You've got a deal," he said.

CHAPTER THIRTEEN

I n August 1923 President Harding died of a stroke and Calvin
Coolidge succeeded him. By November of the next year, the stock
market boom approached a five-year high. On the one hand, Seth
was jubilant. On the other, he felt a gnawing uneasiness despite his
stocks' excellent performance. He had been getting richer by the day.

As they sat in the parlor of Rosie's boardinghouse, Seth looked
at his now pregnant wife. She looked radiant, obviously happy, and
in good health. Still, he couldn't shake a gnawing worry about the
economy. On December 28, 1924, Rosie's water broke, and she had
been whisked off to the closest local hospital where Father John
appeared.

"How's she doing?"

"Just fine. But my son is being obstinate."

"You know the sex already?"

"Not really, but he better not let me down."

They both laughed.

"Have you been reading about what's happening in Germany?"
Seth asked, referring to Hitler's release from Landsberg Prison on
December 20.

Father John nodded.

"That bastard is going to turn the world upside down. How can
they let this happen? By jailing him they've made him a martyr,"
Seth said.

"He's nothing but a common criminal," Father John said.

"That he is. You mark my words, sooner or later that little bastard will bring us all to war," Seth said.

"You know what I think? I think you've got too much time on your hands, too much opportunity to read about two-bit tyrants like Hitler, Mussolini and Franco who'll be forgotten in a few years."

"Too much time on my hands? You want me to get a job?"

"Yes, I do."

"My answer is quite simple. In the first place, it's nice to be part of the idle rich."

Father John laughed.

"Second, taking care of my fortune *is* a full-time job. And third, there's nothing wrong with being informed even if I don't have a job."

At that moment, the doctor arrived.

"You have a son."

"You see! You see! A boy, just like I promised the good Father here."

He hugged the doctor.

"Oh, excuse me, Doctor. This is Father John, my wife's brother, and a good friend."

Smiling, the doctor shook hands then left.

"What is the name that you and Rosie have decided on?"

"His name will be Brian, that way there'll be no hard feelings from anyone in the family who'll be jealous if we don't name him Charles or John or anyone else in the family tree. We just picked it out of the air."

"Good for you, good for you."

Baby Brian brought a round of good luck. The huge Davidson mansion in Elgin went on the market, as Davidson could no longer afford to maintain it. Seeing this ironic reversal of fortune, Seth swept in and bought the place, marking a high point in his life. *With the help of God*, he thought.

Having always wanted a formal education, in early 1925, Seth was admitted as a student at the University of Chicago where he majored in economics with a minor in English. He enjoyed the commuter ride by train because it gave him an opportunity to read on the way. That same year he had been asked to join a group of men who met regularly for lunch each Thursday at the Chicago University Club—Eli Taggert, Emmet Morris, Philip Kinsey, and Hobart Hutchinson—to discuss the stock market. Taggert and Kinsey were insurance salesmen, Morris and Hutchinson stockbrokers. All, of course, were interested in making money in the market.

"Did you hear that Hitler is publishing his memoir?" Seth asked.

"You mean the one he wrote in prison?" Taggert asked.

"The very same. It's due to be published in July. I've read parts. I still think the little bastard will lead us all into a war," Seth said.

"That can't happen. He's got no real power in Germany," Morris answered.

"Not yet, but you just watch, citizens there regard him as a god," Seth said.

"Even if there is a war, there's no way the United States will get into it," Morris said. "Our policy of isolation is paying off. The stock market is going wild, so much so that we've just broken another trading record. My advice to all concerned is to buy, buy, buy, and not worry about what's happening in Europe."

Morris continued. "It's not so tough. I pick a stock, it goes up, I cash in, then I pick another, it goes up, I cash in again. I'm thinking of retiring."

"You're only twenty-nine years old," Seth laughed.

Because the market kept rising, the luncheon group remained committed to its weekly luncheon schedule. On one occasion, Seth attempted to shift the attention of the group away from expected profits.

"Say, did you guys read about Charles Lindbergh? A transatlantic non-stop flight, now that's the kind of adventure I'd like to have. He landed in May at Bourget Field in Paris."

"Are you kidding? Everyone knows about Lindbergh, and you're welcome to react to adventures like that if you want to," Morris said. "As for me, I'd rather sit at home and count my money and study the adventure that is happening around us."

Seth had grown skeptical of the roaring stock market, in part because of what he saw as an impending war in Europe, and because of the market's overexuberance. He started to become bearish with some of his accumulated wealth, pulling back from owning stocks. Still, his friends remained fully invested.

Even when the market took a plunge in December of 1928, Morris wasn't deterred. "It's a temporary adjustment. Keep buying, have no fear," he had said. It was a precursor of an impending disaster.

Morris had remained all in and had, more than once, asked Seth for loans to buy more stock. Others in the group became less bullish, licking their investment wounds, and heeded Seth's advice to sell at least some of their holdings as a hedge.

By October 24, 1929, known as Black Thursday, the stock market had begun a steep decline. By November 13, prices reached their all-time low for the year. After the market crash, it no longer seemed appropriate for Seth to meet with his investment group. By mid-December, however, all felt that at least one luncheon was a good idea if only to toast Morris, their departed colleague, who had committed suicide at the crash's lowest point.

"How could Morris have let things get that bad?" Seth asked the group.

"Do you realize that thirty billion in stock value was wiped out in just a few days? Like a lot of others, Morris was wiped out," Hutchinson said.

"I'd have loaned him the money, even given him the money to turn things around for him," Seth said.

"Maybe so, but he had nothing left. It was all gone," Kinsey said.

"That's no reason to jump out of a window. What about his wife, his daughters?" Seth asked.

"You don't think about such things when you're falling from the thirteenth floor," Kinsey said.

"As I told you recently, you are the only reason the rest of us aren't splattered on the same pavement," Hutchinson said to Seth.

"Me?"

"Yes, you were so convincing with your arguments about the market that the rest of us followed your lead," Kinsey said.

"We all bailed out in time. Everyone but Morris, that is," Hutchinson said.

The Great Depression transformed countless millionaires into apple peddlers overnight. As for Seth, however, his fortune continued to flourish. He was sitting on lots of cash and within three years was back in the market having significantly increased his holdings. Over the same period, he was blessed with two daughters, Jessica, and Jennifer.

In the spring of 1934, Seth stopped by Alphonsus Church.

"I've got everything going for me, Father John, but the Black Dog keeps nipping at my heels."

"Your moods again?"

"Yes, only this time it's worse than ever. I don't want to do anything or go anywhere. I'm driving Rosie nuts."

"What do you think is causing it?"

"I don't know, but I had the same feeling before the stock market crashed—a foreboding, a premonition that something bad is going to happen," Seth said.

"You're right! Something bad is going to happen. That crazy corporal is going to bring the world to war, as you predicted. You probably know they made him chancellor."

"Of course, but Hitler isn't the source of my dread. It's something else, something I can't explain, "Seth said.

"Perhaps you need to broaden your religious commitment. Your children still haven't been christened, and you haven't been baptized."

"We've been delaying those events pending an opportunity to discuss certain matters with you."

"What do you want to tell me?"

"Father John, I haven't been comfortable with the Catholic faith for some time now—the idea of confession, once a week, the pope in Rome, the saints, Purgatory—it doesn't work for me anymore."

"I won't try to dissuade you. How does Rosie feel?"

"Rosie will never leave the Catholic church."

"What denomination have you chosen?"

"Presbyterian."

"I respect that, so long as you keep pursuing your faith after the change is made."

"I intend to."

"What about the children?"

"They can be whatever they want to be when they're old enough to decide. While they're young, Rosie will raise them as Catholics."

"Where's your new church located?"

"In Elgin, the First Presbyterian Church."

"Paul Ewald's the pastor there. I'm aware of his reputation. He's a fine man and an excellent preacher. His church is thriving."

"Rosie's agreed to have our brood baptized there. I'll take the plunge at that time, too. After that, she'll take them regularly to the Catholic church."

"When will all of this be taking place?"

"In two weeks."

"I'd offer to be present, but Catholic priests turn to stone inside Protestant churches."

They laughed.

"Your brother Charles will stand in for you. He's agreed to be godfather," Seth said.

By 1934, the economy had improved with the GNP rising 7.7 percent and unemployment falling to 21.7 percent. Most Americans believed that President Roosevelt's New Deal was working. To most it seemed like the long road to recovery had arrived. In fact, the signs were positive enough to encourage Seth's luncheon group to resume their meetings.

In their regular room, Seth spoke to a Jewish waiter serving the soup course.

"Golan, how are things in the old country?"

"To be Jewish in Germany these days isn't good for one's health. How do I know? My relatives have been able to smuggle a few letters out. We read of lost property rights, arrests, murders."

None of the four knew what to say in response. Unaware that conditions had gotten that bad, all were stunned. When Golan left the room, silence prevailed. With war approaching in Europe, Seth could think of only one thing: *How can I get over there as quickly as possible?*

CHAPTER FOURTEEN

The Reverend Paul F. Ewald, senior pastor of the First Presbyterian Church of Elgin, became Seth Shaw's newest confidant and friend. Ewald at the age of thirty-five had already developed a reputation as a great preacher. Brilliant and articulate, he could hold any congregation spellbound on any given Sunday. With jet black hair and pronounced good looks, Ewald kept the women in the congregation enchanted. With a doctorate in philosophy, Rev. Ewald became the perfect mentor for Seth, who always seemed to be wrestling with deep, restless feelings. They'd been meeting once a week in the reverend's church office for about a month.

"How's Rosie holding up?"

"Very well. I don't know how she puts up with me."

"You're not such a bad sort, and you've got all that money."

Seth ignored the attempt at humor. "You've got to help me, preacher. The Black Dog is destroying me."

"You may not like my suggested remedy, but I'm going to give it to you anyway. In my view, you've got to get a job as soon as possible. I feel that you've got too much free time on your hands. The Black Dog looks for idle hands."

"It comes whether I'm busy or not, and my depression is always followed by manic activity."

"I still think that having a job will help you and I also think you should connect with a newspaper."

"You can't be serious."

"I'm quite serious. What's more, I have secured you a position with the Paris office of the *Chicago Tribune*, if you want to take it."

"You're kidding."

"No, I'm not. It's an ideal time to be in Europe."

"Maybe so, but a newspaper like the *Tribune* is not going to want a person of advanced age and no background in journalism."

"Not so. Newspapers have become more open-minded when a prospective candidate is willing to purchase an interest in the paper for a significant sum of money."

The minister smiled coyly.

"You've already worked out the details, haven't you?" Seth asked.

"I'm afraid so. A relative of the paper's owner is a member of our congregation. The *Tribune* needs investors to stay afloat."

"So that's it."

"Look, you're not exactly a zero when it comes to foreign affairs. More important, you've got the money to cover your own expenses."

"Okay, okay. What's the first step?"

"Next Tuesday at two you're scheduled to meet with Colonel Robert R. McCormick who heads the Paris bureau of the *Tribune*, better known as the *Paris Tribune*. Everyone refers to him as the Colonel."

"Do I meet him in Paris?"

"No, in Chicago. It's not an interview; you've got the job, so long as you're willing to make an investment of twenty-five thousand dollars."

At the scheduled time, Seth arrived at Colonel McCormick's office and was admitted immediately. There was a large world map on one wall with colored pins in place. The Colonel looked small behind his gigantic desk backed by the gigantic map.

"Mr. Shaw, do you think you can buy your way into this newspaper?"

"Well—"

"You've got no experience, you don't speak French, you know

nothing about foreign affairs, you've never written a news story in your life. Why on earth should I hire you?"

Still standing, Seth moved a step closer.

"For one thing, no newspaper person could ever find a more exciting time in history to be working overseas. War is coming. You'll need many enthusiastic correspondents to keep up with it."

"Why should you be one of them?"

"The seams are splitting in several places. You'll need to have coverage in all of them, Hitler in Germany, Mussolini in Italy, Franco in Spain. And don't forget Japan. It's all going to explode very soon whether it's weeks, months or years depends on how efficiently and effectively those bastards can work. And no one is going to stop them—no one—once they get going . . . at least not right away. Any newspaperman who isn't aware of these things should resign. Also, Colonel, twenty-five thousand dollars is a lot of money."

"Don't be so negative, Mr. Shaw. Consider how far civilization has come. Over time we've come up with a host of new ways to kill people." Colonel McCormick laughed.

Seth stepped back slightly.

"Mr. Shaw, I've been putting you on. Have a seat. I agree with your analysis, and I like your grit. You've got the job, and you can report as soon as you're able, in Paris. Call me Colonel and I'll call you Seth, if you don't mind. By the way, I don't give a rat's ass whether my reporters can speak the language or not. In fact, I prefer it when they can't. That way they don't become embroiled in local politics."

He and Seth worked out the formal arrangements on the spot and Seth wrote a check. The Colonel explained that he visited Paris twice a year for the biannual operational meeting held at the Ritz. He sensed that his Paris staff hated these encounters, but he liked the role of tyrant and felt his presence sparked productivity, adding that he must get the best out of what little staff was left.

"The Depression has hit the paper hard," he said. "Your investment will help keep the lights on a little bit longer. For that, I thank you."

By the time all travel arrangements had been made, another month had passed. The ship on which Rosie and Seth and their children sailed was scheduled to arrive at Le Havre. During an uneventful crossing, the three children had an opportunity to sleep most of the way. When they arrived by train to Paris, a *Tribune* employee was waiting, holding a sign with the paper's name on it.

"Hello, I'm Reginald Pierce," he said. "Everybody calls me Reg. Sometimes French trains are on time, but mostly they're not. We were lucky this time."

Seth introduced his family: Rosie, Brian, Jessica, and Jennifer. The little girls, both under the age of five, giggled. Young Brian, who was older, glared at them. As they walked to the car, Reg commented about his role.

"I'm supposed to spy on you, act as the paper's watchdog, that sort of thing. But I'm going to scratch all that and just be your friend."

"Thank you."

They all boarded Reg's car for a ride to the hotel.

"Since you're low on publishing experience I suggest that you and I plan to have breakfast regularly until you've had the opportunity to learn the ropes."

"That's very kind of you," Seth said.

"Think nothing of it. I was given similar help when I arrived in Paris six years ago, and I've always wanted to return the favor. I understand your stay at the Ritz is temporary until you find something suitable."

"That's correct," Rosie said. "We'll rent or buy, it doesn't matter. We're also looking for a governess for the children, if you have any ideas."

"Not at the moment, but I'll put some thought to it."

"I guess you've met our worthy leader?" Reg asked.

"You mean the Colonel?"

"Yes. His bark is worse than his bite. He likes to play tyrant, claims to know where the news is going to break before it happens, but he's very often wrong. But we don't remind him of that. He's got a big job. Times are tough at the paper. Circulation has fallen off greatly. As a matter of fact, you might get some dirty looks."

"Why is that?"

"The staff will be thinking that the Colonel is paying you in salary what they should be getting in bonuses."

"I see."

"Oh, look," Rosie said. "There's the Eiffel Tower."

As he drove, Reg gave sightseeing suggestions including the advisability of a trip to France's famous landmark that they were passing at the time. Shortly, he found a spot on the circular driveway in front of the Ritz and moved ahead to help with the luggage, some of which had been sent ahead by cab. Even though he wasn't expected to report for work until the following Monday, Seth arrived in the office the very next day.

That evening he returned home full of enthusiasm.

"Rosie, it's incredible. Everyone is so nice to me, not one dirty look. The place sounds like a sawmill—ringing phones, shouted orders, pounding typewriters. I love it, and many reporters came to my small cubicle to introduce themselves, famous reporters who could scoop me one hundred times a day. I've already gotten my first assignment."

"Darling, that's wonderful. The children and I have been out walking. We had a fantastic time, too."

To Rosie, Paris was clearly the most beautiful city in the world, and most important, a place where Seth would be happy. The children had seemed to recognize that the city offered wonderful new things to enjoy. Jessica and Jennifer gathered round their father to report on their adventures. Young Brian sat in a chair pretending to read a magazine.

"Listen, babe, you and I are going to Maxim's. Reg has made a reservation on our behalf several weeks ago. Apparently, the Colonel has some swat there."

"What about the children?"

"Reg's mother-in-law is coming over. If we like her, she's offered to take on the job of governess."

"Oh, that's perfect," Rosie said.

"Put on your best dress, babe, and we'll let the champagne flow."

As Seth dressed, he noticed that the Black Dog had left him. Perhaps Reverend Ewald's strategy was working after all. At first, he felt guilty about sweeping the family into a new environment. No more. Everyone seemed happy, buoying Seth even more.

Maxim's proved to be everything the critics had promised. They sat at a table with one lighted candle in place. As he studied her in the flickering candlelight—the sexy dress she had selected, the dark eyes sparkling, the lustrous sweep of her black hair, and most exciting, the smile showing pearly-white teeth over lipstick-red lips—he became aroused. Her eyes expressed happiness and love. He stared transfixed. No words came. Finally, he put his hand forward and touched hers.

"Do you know how much I love you?" he asked.

"Yes, I know because I have the same feelings."

They finished a bottle of excellent champagne that produced a giddiness in both, a condition that became evident when they attempted to stand. That night they made perfect love. The next day Seth remembered that he had secured letters of introduction from the Colonel to Sylvia Beach and Gertrude Stein.

"Reg tells me that Hemingway used the same tactic years before with the help of Sherwood Anderson," Seth said.

"What's good enough for Hemingway is certainly good enough for us," Rosie laughed.

Knowing how much Seth admired Hemingway, Rosie had developed an interest of her own.

"I can't wait to meet Sylvia Beach," he said.

"Who's Sylvia Beach?"

Seth explained that years ago Sylvia championed the idea of opening a bookstore and lending library for Americans in Paris. She saw to it that the books were available in English for the ever-increasing contingent of expatriates. After naming her bookstore Shakespeare & Company, she found a perfect initial location, which had worked well until she moved to the current location on the Rue de L'Odéon. Rosie and Seth decided to walk there from the hotel. Seth had called previously to tell Sylvia they were coming.

"She's got to be a character," Rosie said as they walked.

"Sylvia's quite brilliant and knows her trade well, with lots of contacts, mostly artists and writers, all of whom seem to like and respect her very much. By the way, Sylvia has a relationship with a woman by the name Adrienne Monnier."

"You mean the two are—"

"Yes, they live together. Adrienne will probably be there."

"I'm glad you told me."

"Keep in mind that Shakespeare & Company is the original publisher of James Joyce's *Ulysses*, which says a lot about Sylvia."

Sylvia and Adrienne were both waiting in the doorway when they arrived. Adrienne, a mountain of a woman and matronly, was dressed in an officer's waistcoat tightly buttoned at the neck over a long, ankle-length skirt. Small and thin and four years older than Adrienne, Sylvia wore a velvet smoking jacket complimented by a flowing red tie. Her eyes were bright and brown. She had boyishly bobbed hair brushed back from her forehead and cut thick below the ears.

"Do you speak the language?" Adrienne asked.

"We're working on it," Rosie said.

"But none too successfully," Seth laughed.

"It's always wonderful to have visitors and Adrienne and I do love Americans," Sylvia said. "Please come in. We're hoping you'll join us for lunch. The shop is closed for the occasion."

"We'd be delighted," Rosie answered.

Seth's mind wandered as he walked toward a luncheon table in the center of a large room dominated by bookshelves. A tablecloth was spread out to accommodate wine glasses, plates, and silverware already in place. The atmosphere was cozy in the restricted space, the room dominated by tall shelves containing books interrupted only by thin leaded windows between each bookcase.

"We're both good cooks," Sylvia said. "But we prefer using a caterer when we're serving lunch or dinner here at the bookstore. André does a wonderful job. Besides, there are no facilities here that would permit us to cook with any degree of success. Ah, here's André now."

André presented an exquisite lunch that included an excellent pâté plus an assortment of cheeses on a wooden platter with slices of duck, turkey and chicken thinly sliced. Almost as an afterthought were two baskets of French bread and two bottles of wine, one white and one red. When all had eaten their fill, the conversation shifted to various topics, including the Shaw children, cities of origin for Seth and Rosie, night spots and restaurants in Paris, and the Maxim experience. Coffee was served in delicate demitasses.

"Adrienne's bookstore is nearby," Sylvia said. "Hers, of course, caters to a French clientele. She's probably the first woman in Paris to open such a bookstore."

"Oh, Sylvia, you do go on," Adrienne said. "You two certainly picked the best time of year to come to Paris. The chestnuts are in blossom. The smells are wonderful. I'll take April in Paris over any other month."

"I understand that Hemingway has come here often, to your bookstore I mean," Seth said.

"Indeed, he has," Sylvia answers.

"What's he like?" Rosie asked.

"He has always been nice to me, but he can be difficult. He has turned against several of his friends—Sherwood Anderson, Gertrude Stein, Scott Fitzgerald, Ezra Pound—to name a few. Despite all of that, I like him, consider him a close friend. He's a genius, you know. When you're a genius, you can get away with a lot."

"It's more than that," Seth said. "He's a symbol, an icon, a man's man. Look at his favorite activities—hunting, bull fighting, boxing, deep sea fishing, skiing—all the while writing the greatest American literature ever written."

"I'm not so crazy about his novels," Sylvia said, "but many of his short stories are masterpieces—*Snows of Kilimanjaro, A Short Happy Life, My Old Man.*"

"I agree totally," Rosie said, "except I'd add *The Killers* to the list."

"I see we have another Hemingway aficionado among us." Sylvia said.

"There is a greatness in most of the things he's written. Still, there are certain aspects of his character that are deplorable," Rosie said.

"Go on."

"Well, for one thing he's a drunk," Rosie continued. "For another, he uses and discards women like dirty laundry. He's got a mean streak and he turns on friends without warning. He's also a chauvinist. On the bottom line, there's something that doesn't ring true about him. He tries too hard to project his macho image," Rosie said.

"Would you call him a phony?" Sylvia asked.

"Definitely," Rosie said.

"Yet, you're fascinated by him?" Sylvia said.

"I suppose I am."

The topic shifted.

"I understand from the Colonel that you'd like to meet Gertrude Stein. I'm very flattered that you think I have a connection with her, but, unfortunately, I won't be able to help you. Our relationship has soured. It happened after I agreed to publish Joyce's work. From then on Gertrude has been very cool toward me. I suppose she thinks I'm a turncoat."

"A turncoat?" Rosie asked.

"Yes, you must understand that when it comes to egos, Gertrude is no slacker. She puts herself on a par with Joyce—even Shakespeare. My decision to publish Joyce's work was to her a slap in the face."

"I've never read any of her books. In fact, before this trip, I'd never even heard of her," Rosie said.

"She does have a following, and she's quite charming. Nevertheless, I'd think twice about going with Seth to meet her. Because of her pomposity, she likes to separate the men from the women who are palmed off on Alice—Alice B. Toklas, her friend and lover."

"When Seth schedules a meeting, I'll fake a cold and miss it," Rosie said.

They all laugh.

"Wait a minute. I can't meet with her just yet. I haven't read any of her books," Seth added.

"When are you scheduled to meet with her?"

"I haven't set anything up yet, but I'm shooting for next Saturday."

"Good I'll give you two or three of her novels to read in the interim."

Rosie and Seth said their goodbyes and began the journey back to the Ritz.

"Rosie, are you sure you don't want to meet Gertrude?" Seth said as they walked.

"I'd rather choke to death, thank you."

"That's your call. By the way, I wish you wouldn't be so critical of Hemingway. You know how much I admire him."

"I'm allowed to have my own views."

Rosie stopped walking.

"You're always talking about Hitler and Mussolini. In my view Hemingway is cut from the same cloth. In all cases, it's the male ego run amok, the idea of proving great strength, survival of the fittest . . . that sort of thing. Hemingway hooks fish and blows game away. The tyrants chop up people and blow countries away. There's not much difference really, just a matter of degree," she said.

"There's all the difference in the world. You won't go to jail for bagging quail or catching trout," he said.

"Whenever a person begins to think he's infallible, there's one hell of a price to pay both on a small scale and a large one. And it's not just a male thing. Look at Catherine the Great of Russia," Rosie said.

"I had no idea you felt this way."

"Well, I do. Consider that relative of yours in Skagway. He got full of himself; thought he was smarter than everyone else."

"Soapy Smith?"

"Yes, and he ended up dead. That's what happens to people like that and it's going to happen to Hitler and Mussolini. You watch . . . the war will end in destruction for both. Hubris. Hubris is the culprit," she said.

The following Monday, Seth and Reg had breakfast at the Ritz.

"As far as the job is concerned, just express a willingness to take on anything they might want to assign to you and you'll do fine," Reg said. "You're doing great already, I might add. I'm getting input from a lot of different sources, all positive. Keep up the good work and you'll thrive."

"When is the Colonel coming?"

"Hasn't set a date yet."

"What's it like working for him?"

"He does like to have his own way. He can make a reporter's life pure misery if he wants to. Many a correspondent at the *Paris Tribune* lost their job because of him, and his whims."

"I'll keep that in mind."

"Don't kid me, Seth. You're a multi-millionaire. You don't need this job. You could care less."

"I do care, but on the issue of finances, please spread the word that my presence in Paris hasn't put anyone's bonus in jeopardy. On the contrary, I've invested twenty-five thousand dollars in the paper, and I've insisted that no salary be paid to me until I can carry my own weight. Six months should give me enough time to learn the ropes."

That evening, Seth and Rosie planned to attend a dinner party at the residence of the American ambassador, Seth in tuxedo and Rosie in evening dress.

"Darling, you look so beautiful. I'm weak at the knees."

She smiled, pleased that his disposition had improved greatly since their arrival in Paris, convinced he was a new person chiefly because of his new position. His work at the *Tribune* had lifted the gloom, the Black Dog, so much so, in fact, that he was able to make love to her regularly again.

There was a knock at the door. Mimi, Reg's mother-in-law, had come to take care of the children.

"Where are my munchkins?" she asked prompting the two little girls to come squealing to her as she stood in the doorway.

"Here they are, my two little fairies."

Their brother watched from a distance.

"How's my big boy?"

"I'm okay," young Brian snorted.

Mimi was sober and austere, saying little and smiling less except when relating to the children when she was effusive and full of laughter. Seth guessed that she may have been dealing with her own Black Dog. In her late fifties, divorced, Mimi was disinterested in men, confirmed by her disheveled appearance showing unruly grey hair, and clothes that were often spotted and wrinkled that and did not fit. She drove an old car that was always unwashed and filled with debris.

"She seems so sad, so unhappy," Seth said as he and Rosie drove off. "I expect she's going through a period of depression."

"She's devoted to the children, though, and that's what counts," Rosie said.

"Reg tells me that her family once had lots of money, most of which passed to her. He also advises that she received a handsome divorce settlement. I expect he wants us to know that she doesn't need the money," Seth said.

"I'm sure she took the job because of the children. Her full name is Helene Duchamp. She's a French national. Best of all, she is only ten minutes away," Rosie said.

When they returned from the dinner party, Mimi was waiting.

"I have the most wonderful news," Mimi said, "A house has come up for sale that will be perfect for you."

She produced a hand-drawn map, explaining that the house, which she described as a villa, was just eight miles outside of Paris.

"It's owned by one of my relatives. They're being transferred to the States. I spoke to them tonight."

"On Saturday I'm scheduled to visit Gertrude Stein in the morning. Do you think we could set up something in the afternoon?" Seth said.

"I'll try."

After Mimi left, Seth and Rosie discussed the villa further.

"I hope Mimi is on to something. I'm tired of living in a hotel room," Seth said.

"I know she's going to pull this off. I have one of my feelings," she said.

"I hope your feeling is accurate," he said.

He removed his tie and draped it on the tie rack.

"Babe, I don't know why we go to affairs like that one. They're always so boring."

"Get used to it. The American ambassador is an important man here in France. Without his influence, Brian would never have gotten into Marymount. Besides, it's a chance to wear fancy clothes," she said.

"According to Reg, the Colonel contacted the ambassador one day after I accepted the job. The Colonel, he said, is of the view that when it comes to restaurants and schooling, it is best to pull strings early."

The day following the notice of acceptance at Marymount, Seth took Brian on a walk along the Seine.

"I hope you're excited about the prospect of attending Marymount. It's a wonderful school. We pulled strings to get you in there—a lot of strings. This is your first real test, and I'm counting on you to come through."

"Will my classes be taught in French?" Brian asked.

"No, that's the beauty of it. French will be offered, but only in a separate class."

"Will I be a day student?"

"Yes, I'll travel with you by train into Paris, and they'll have a bus waiting for you there."

On the river a barge passed. They both stopped to watch until it disappeared in the distance.

"Brian?"

"Yes."

"As your father, I've got to confess some things to you."

They begin walking again.

"I haven't been a very good father—"

"Dad . . . I—"

"No, let me finish. In addition to being very busy at work, I'm also affected by what I call the Black Dog, which is a disorder that causes depression as well as mania. The result of all of this is that I haven't been able to spend as much time with you as I would have liked. I'm sorry."

"Dad, you don't need to tell me all of this. I know you've done your best."

Seth stopped again.

"I tell you this, as a warning. This ugly condition is genetic, which means that it may affect you, so I want you to keep track of your emotions. The first moment you begin to feel depressed I want you to tell me."

"Dad, I've already had those feelings."

CHAPTER FIFTEEN

O n Saturday, Seth traveled alone to Gertrude Stein's studio
at 27 Rue de Fleurus and knocked on one of two large
double doors in front. Almost immediately the door
opened, revealing a lanky woman with straight black hair and a
prominent nose.

"Mr. Shaw, I'm Alice Toklas. Please follow me."

Alice looked downright homely and thin as a reed. Her hair was
disheveled with wisps of grey. She had a side-to-side gait, which
indicated that her feet were giving her problems. Inside, the studio
looked like an art salon. Paintings were hung everywhere. Alice
introduced Seth to Gertrude, who was lying on a chaise lounge
looking enormous and regal, dressed in a corduroy outfit with a skirt
long enough to cover her ankles. Her close-cropped hair was the
same pale red as the outfit she was wearing. Red bedroom slippers
completed the ensemble. She didn't seem the least bit embarrassed
by her excessive weight.

"I would have greeted you myself, but I'm suffering from a touch
of gout," Gertrude said.

"That's quite alright. It gave me an opportunity to meet Alice,"
Seth said as he sat.

"Well, aren't you a charmer, and handsome, too. May we offer
you some coffee or wine?" Gertrude asked.

"Coffee, please, if you have some made."

"Coming right up," Alice said.

"Tell me about yourself," Gertrude said.

"Not much to tell. Born in San Francisco, grew up in Elgin, Illinois, inherited a fortune, bribed the *Paris Tribune* into hiring me, came here."

"Aren't you leaving a few details out?"

"Like what?" Seth smiled.

"Your occupation as a bouncer in a New Orleans house of ill repute, your connection with a crime family in Chicago, and your escape from an assassination attempt at Rivoli's Restaurant."

"You certainly have done your homework."

"You see, even though we aren't part of the press, we still have ways of getting information. What have you found out about us?"

"Let's see, Radcliffe, then Harvard, several books, numerous lectures, extensive connections in the literary world, a deep appreciation of art—"

"Have you read any of my books?"

"As a matter of fact, yes. I've read *Three Lives* and *The Autobiography of Alice B. Toklas*. Both, by the way, are excellent."

"Well, thank you."

Alice returned with coffee for Seth, and Gertrude changed the subject.

"Are you aware of the fact that Alice and I are both Jewish?"

"I am."

"In your view, should we be concerned here in France, considering the state of affairs in Germany?"

"In my view, we all should be concerned. The lunatics have taken over the asylum. War is inevitable."

"How soon?" Gertrude asked.

"Most likely 1939 at the latest. There is no holding that madman back now."

"Mr. Shaw, you seem like an intelligent man, but on this point you're totally wrong. There will be no war," Gertrude said.

"Why do you say that?"

"Mussolini hasn't got the strength and Hitler is a romantic. When it gets right down to it, he'll avoid war."

"I hope you're right. I'm not concerned for myself. I've been around long enough, but my children, well—"

"I certainly hope I'm right. When a Jew dies, he's dead, that's the end of it," she said.

Seth bowed his head, reluctant to challenge her beliefs.

"Have you noticed the painting above my head?" she asked.

"Yes, I've been admiring it."

"It is an abstract portrait of me done by Picasso several years ago. My brother Leo thinks it's horrible."

"Your brother Leo is wrong."

For the next hour, the three discussed art and art history. Gertrude was particularly fond of Cézanne. The conversation then shifted to the wonders of Paris, and finally to Hemingway. Seth knew there was bad blood between Gertrude and Ernest but didn't press for details.

"Mr. Shaw, Alice and I would like you to come to a cocktail party here during the last week of April. She'll hand you a written invitation. Please bring your wife."

Alice handed him the invitation, which signaled the visit was over.

In the late afternoon, Reg and Mimi arrived to take Seth and Rosie to see the house available for purchase.

"Now don't hold back," Reg said while driving. "Let's hear everything concerning Queen Gertrude?"

"You know, I was just telling Rosie that she's a character and a half, with a regal bearing. As much as I'm tempted to dislike her, I can't do it. She's very charming."

"Go on," Reg said.

"Well, she's obviously brilliant—"

"And lets you know it in no uncertain terms," Reg interrupted.

"I suppose that's true, but one doesn't mind because she's correct in that assessment."

"Tell me more."

"Well, I'd say she's totally comfortable in her own skin—"

"Even though there's an awful lot of it," Reg said, laughing.

"Reggie, please quit interrupting." Mimi scolded.

"One thing I can tell you for sure is that Sylvia Beach saved my bacon," Seth said.

"How so?"

"She gave me two of Gertrude's books to read before going over there. The flattery must have worked because she invited Rosie and me to a party . . . during the last week of April."

"Oh, no," Rosie said.

"You shouldn't feel that way, Rosie," Reg said. "Anyone who is anybody in the art world will be there. You don't want to miss it."

"Don't worry, we won't," Seth said. "I've already accepted . . . for both of us.

"One thing amazes me, as smart as she is and as well informed as she is, she doesn't believe there will be a war. She should know better, the handwriting is on the wall," Seth said.

"Oh, look, there's the house," Mimi said.

Reg slowed so that they all could see.

"I suppose you can describe it as a villa," Mimi said.

"Looks wonderful from the outside," Rosie said.

The house had everything Rosie and Seth were looking for—a courtyard, a circular driveway, four large bedrooms upstairs, and two smaller ones on the first floor, each with a view of the courtyard outside. It also offered a huge kitchen and oversized dining and living areas. Hardwood floors and cream-colored stucco walls were consistent throughout. They discussed the house on the way back.

"You know what I liked most, the casement windows. I love great quantities of light," Rosie said.

"I'll tell you what I loved, the huge kitchen. It's perfect—not that I plan to do any cooking," Seth said.

They all laughed.

"Mimi, we'll want you to come live with us. You can give up your apartment and take the bedroom in the attic," Rosie said.

"I'm flattered. I'll think on it."

They closed on the purchase the following week. By the time of Gertrude's party, they had moved in.

The party was humming when they arrived. Rosie had insisted on arriving early so that they could leave early without raising hackles. Rosie and Seth were immediately struck by the disparity in dress. A man wore a red and white striped T-shirt and red shorts complimented by a red scarf and sandals, a woman was in what appeared to be a toga sucking on a long cigarette holder, another was in a low-backed dress and another in a flowered kimono. Berets were everywhere, along with the customary black outfits favored by both sexes. A few men were in suits and ties, but not many. The music of a Spanish guitarist filled the room.

Seth spotted Gertrude and introduced Rosie.

"Aren't you concerned that someone might run off with one of your fabulous paintings?" Rosie asked Gertrude.

"That's what Iggy is for."

She pointed to a huge man in a black outfit on the far side of the room.

"You should know that there are some very interesting people here," Gertrude said.

It was difficult to hear her over the noise and Seth didn't catch the names.

"I'll ask Alice to bring that crazy Spaniard over here to meet you and keep an eye on you. He speaks English, but not very well."

She beckoned to Alice who then brought the man over.

"Let me introduce you to two Americans."

"Do you know my work?" asked Pablo Picasso.

"Of course. We've both heard a lot about you," Rosie said.

The Spaniard smiled.

"Now this lady the one who makes the party, she thinks she be genius, thinks her Pupa doesn't stink. All I know is she be smart enough to buy my paintings. That is genius enough for me."

Picasso belted out a high-pitched squeal. Seth was struck by his penetrating eyes and solid build.

"Do you know her latest brilliant idea?" he asked.

"What's that?" Seth asked.

"Our esteemed hostess thinks that Hitler should win Nobel Peace Prize."

"She can't be serious," Rosie said.

"Ah, but she is. If you eliminate the Communists and the Jews, she said, who is left to fight with?"

He belted out another squeal of laughter.

"That's certainly one way to look at it," Seth said, smiling, growing increasingly uncomfortable with the famous painter.

When Alice reappeared, Seth was relieved.

"I've got an American you should meet," she said. "Gertrude and I call him Kiddie. We've known him for years. His real name is William G. Rogers, a reporter for the *Springfield, Massachusetts Union*. Let me introduce you."

The crazy Spaniard disappeared into the crowd. After Alice left, Rosie, Seth, and Rogers found a couch where they could talk.

"You know, we're lucky," Rogers said.

"Why is that?" Rosie asked.

"Under normal circumstances, by late April they'd be gone to their summer place in Bilignin."

"Bilignin? Where's that?" Rosie asked.

"Southeast France, not far from Mont Blanc. I've never been

there, but they've asked me to join them this year just as soon as they get settled in. I've seen pictures. It's idyllic—tiled roof, shuttered windows, courtyard below, that sort of thing."

"Why it sounds very much like the villa we just purchased outside Paris." Rosie said.

"How do you come to know Alice and Gertrude?" Seth asked.

He explained that while doing some sightseeing on furlough in 1917, he met them at the Luxembourg Hotel.

"They befriend me, and we begin sightseeing together."

"Why do they call you Kiddie?" Rosie asked.

"Just a nickname."

He explained that they were very kind to include him on their sightseeing tour to Arles, Avignon, and Orange where they saw Roman ruins, and Romanesque churches, all the while stopping to sleep at inns and to eat at roadside stops.

"It was great fun, and do you know they never let me pay for a thing. They're quite generous."

"And you haven't seen them in all that time?" Rosie asked.

"Not until today."

"So, Seth, what do you do?" Rogers continued.

"I'm a foreign correspondent with the *Paris Tribune*."

"Impressive."

"Maybe not," Seth corrected. "I inherited a lot of money, which is probably a curse although it permitted me to buy a position on the paper."

"There's nothing wrong with that. Everybody needs a start."

"Yes, I thought a fresh start would eliminate my glum moods but whatever I do, I can't shake the feeling of impending doom that has come over me recently. I call it the Black Dog."

"Now, darling, I'm sure Mr. Rogers doesn't want to hear about all of that," Rosie said.

"It's quite alright. We all have skeletons in our closets," Rogers said.

"We must be going. It was a pleasure to meet you," Rose said.

They thanked Alice and Gertrude for the invitation and headed back to the car.

"I really liked Bill Rogers." Seth said.

"Yes, so did I."

The months passed quickly. With Reg's help, Seth became a respected member of the *Paris Tribune's* staff. He reported for work regularly at the main office at 5 Rue Lamartine at a worksite on the Right Bank shared with a French daily, *Le Petit Journal*. Anyone coming to work had to climb three flights, a feat that arguably screened out drunks and vagrants. Seth soon discovered that, despite the stairway challenge, several newspaper staffers routinely showed up to work inebriated.

The capable and well-liked managing editor, Ralph Jules Frantz, had been with the paper since 1925. Sage as he was with great news instincts, he occasionally pursued a bad idea, as Seth soon learned.

"Shaw, I want you to do a piece on the Maginot Line. Do you know what that is?"

"Of course."

"Yes, well, I want you to go out there and study it. Find out if it's any good."

"Let's think about that, chief. The French have built a line of defense hundreds of miles long, spent a lot of money on it, a structure on a par with the Great Wall of China, except that most of it is underground where there is access to railway lines and troop barracks and guns and more guns."

"What's your point?"

"Do you think they're going to let me get within a hundred miles of it?"

"Well—"

"And if there is a vulnerability—and there probably is a

vulnerability—do you think that they'll want me to report on it in the paper?"

Pause.

"You're correct. Scrap the Maginot Line idea. Do a piece on Josephine Baker instead."

"Chief, now you're talking."

Seth expected to find the famous dancer and singer easily, but soon learned of Josephine's aloofness. Despite the difficulty, he intensely researched her background, relying on the library for news clippings and other background materials, all the while making extensive notes:

Real name: *Freda Josephine McDonald*

Stage name: *Josephine Baker*

Other names*: Black Venus, Black Pearl, Creole Goddess*

Place of Birth*: St. Louis, Missouri*

Awards*: Queen of the Colonial Exposition of 1931*

Writings*: Les Mémoires des Joséphine Baker*

Films*: Zou-Zou (1934), Princesse Tam-Tam (1935)*

Current residence*: Beau-Chêne, a château located in Le Vésinet, a Paris suburb.*

Fanciful Ethnic Background: *A descendant of Apalachee Indians and Black slaves in South Carolina.*

Actual Ethnic Background: *Fathered by a Jewish salesman.*

Career: Saint Louis—*Started dancing in the streets as a child before joining the Chorus at age fifteen.*

Career: New York City—*Performed at the Plantation Club in Harlem and in the chorus of certain popular Broadway revues: "Shuffle Along" (1921) and "The Chocolate Dandies" (1924).*

Career: Paris—*Opened at the Théâtre des Champs-Élysées on October 2, 1925; graduated to the Folies-Bergère; also performed at*

Chez Joséphine. After a successful tour of Europe, she returned to star at the Casino de Paris, a music hall.

Countries seen on tour: *Austria, Rumania, Hungary, Spain, Germany, Denmark, Sweden, Norway, Holland, Columbia, Uruguay, Brazil, Chile.*

The remaining background was gathered from interviews with various employees who knew her at *the Théâtre des Champs-Élysées* and the *Folies Bergère.* A former night watchman at one theatre remembered her well and didn't mince words. "Oh, you should have seen her. That brown skin, that exotic face—she likes to appear practically naked. Even if you think you've seen exotic dancing, you haven't seen exotic dancing until you've seen her."

A manager at the same theater was equally as effusive.

"She performs wearing only high heels and a skirt made of bananas."

"Did you say bananas?"

"Bananas, as in the fruit. She is often accompanied by her pet cheetah."

"You've got to be kidding."

"Might be a leopard, come to think of it, by the name of Chiquita. Wears a diamond collar." He laughed. "I can't tell you how many times that animal escaped into the orchestra pit. Drives the musicians nuts."

"I can imagine."

Seth stopped in at Frantz's office.

"Chief, I still haven't tracked her down, yet, but I'm getting a very positive picture before actually meeting her."

"Oh?"

"I like her already. Rose from nothing to become the main attraction in glittering Paris. That isn't too shabby when you think about it, and it hasn't gone to her head from what I hear. Rumor is that she has some thirteen pets. You don't have thirteen animals unless you have a warm heart."

"Seth, you're taking too long on this. I need your piece by the end of the week."

"But Chief, I can't do a write-up without an interview."

"By now you should have done that. She's involved in two films. Maybe you can find her through her producer. He's right here in Paris."

Seth tracked her down the next day and scheduled an interview. Just off the set, Josephine wore a thick black robe. The characteristic that struck Seth most was not her caramel-colored skin, but instead her clear, bright eyes. He was also quite taken by her infectious smile.

"You really saved my bacon, Miss Baker. My editor is asking for a finished piece by the end of the week."

"Please call me Josephine . . . and I'm happy to help out."

"Maybe so, but you are very kind to schedule this interview on such short notice."

"You're most welcome, honey."

"Let's start with the most important issue of all. Is Chiquita a leopard or a cheetah?"

Josephine laughed heartily.

"Honey, he's a leopard, a male leopard. Oh, that animal hates to drive with Pepito, who is a lousy driver. So, we send him by cab."

She laughed again.

"You know about Pepito, he acts like my husband, but we never actually married. Still, he manages my career, and he has done a wonderful job of it, too."

"What's his real name?"

She tells him.

"We go back a long way, honey. It's his idea to send me on the European tour. It is perfect timing. The Parisians were getting a little tired of me."

"Tired?"

"Oh, I can sing and dance okay. No one has any problem with any of that. It's just that the act needed to be upgraded. Pepito became convinced that a European tour would accomplish all of that, and it did."

"Tell me more, please."

"When I went on the tour I'm described as a *rough stone,* and when I came back, I'm a 'a polished gem, at least that's what one critic said."

"The critics love you?"

"Honey, let me tell you, it's more than that. Upon my return, all of Paris loved me. I'm the toast of the town."

"You're a different person?"

"Yes. I have new confidence and maturity. My voice reaches a new range and a new sophistication."

"I've been reading those reviews," Seth said. "They all talk about an innocence, a sweetness that you are able to project."

"Pepito has been helping me with that. He has always seen to it that such qualities once in place must not be extinguished."

"What happened on the tour?"

"We went everywhere, at least it seemed that way We were gone for about two and a half years. We got back in April of 1929."

A producer who ran the *Casino de Paris,* hired her to star in the 1930-31 variety show. It went so well that he hired her again for the 1932-33 show. That producer, an admirer, bought her the leopard.

"We became inseparable, that leopard and me."

"Is it true that you have thirteen pets?" Seth asked.

"Fourteen. Just picked up another stray this morning. I can't stand to see any animal suffer."

"What's it like being a big star?"

"Honey, I love it, yes, I love it with all my heart. I'd die if that's what it took to please a crowd."

"You talk about your appearance. Permit me to say that your eyes and your smile are infectious, extravagant, and your body, you must know it's incredible."

"Well, thank you, honey. Blow in my ear and I'll follow you anywhere." She laughed.

"What's it like up there on stage?"

She paused.

"It's like nothing you can imagine. Dancing creates a magic fairyland. If I'm prevented from doing it, I'll wither and die, honestly, I will," she said.

"Tell me about your newest act," Seth said.

"The act at the recent variety show was incredible, truly incredible—a spiral staircase, lots of feathers and yards and yards of gold and silver lamé."

"Go on."

"Critics refer to one dance as 'a sexual rape fantasy.' I appear in a skimpy costume that includes a large pair of diaphanous wings. Abruptly, male dancers appear, half naked, and begin to attack me. The music builds to a crescendo as they rip off my wings."

"That will put a stir in the cheap seats," Seth laughed.

"You've got that right, honey," she said.

"Josephine, what's coming up? After your work on the latest film is completed, what will you do?"

"In the fall of this year, 1934, I'm starring in an opera, *La Creole*. It'll be something new for me. I've never appeared in a Paris theatre as opposed to a music hall . . . what's more I've never sung light opera."

"It'll be my first opportunity to see you dance."

"Please come, I want you to come."

"You live with Pepito?"

"Yes."

"Will you marry him?"

"Probably not."

Seth departed and the piece was published that Friday, just as Ralph Frantz had requested. In the fall of 1934, Seth went to see *La Creole*. At that production he learned first-hand what the fuss was all about. Josephine was fabulous, in all areas: singing, dancing, acting. The audience loved her. The applause at the end was deafening. She took three curtain calls.

CHAPTER SIXTEEN

Mimi had stopped sleeping or eating from the day her physician first diagnosed ovarian cancer after having located a tumor in her abdomen the size of an orange. Mimi gave her doctor strict instructions not to reveal the diagnosis to anyone, including family members.

On the tragic day, Reg, received a phone call from a police officer speaking French.

"I'm afraid, Mr. Pierce, I've got very terrible news for you. Your mother-in-law has killed herself."

Reg was dumbfounded and for several seconds was unable to speak.

"What, what are your saying? Please tell me again.

He did.

I don't know what to say. I can't imagine that she would do such a thing. How did it happen?"

"That's the other part of it," the officer said.

"What do you mean?"

"Well, she didn't just kill herself."

"What? What do you mean? Who else died? For God's sake, who else died?"

"She drove her car into a garage, in a villa, closed the garage door, and left the engine running with the car windows open. Apparently, she worked there as the governess. Unfortunately, the fumes seeped into the children's bedroom above the garage. Both little girls who were sleeping there died."

Reg began to sob as the officer continued.

"Tragically, that's not all. Although the mother of the little girls would probably have survived in her own bedroom, on that night she was sleeping with the little girls. I should also tell you that our initial investigation indicates that the Shaw family deaths are purely accidental. We have every reason to believe that the governess intended to kill only herself."

Reg sobbed, unable to speak, knowing Mimi adored the children.

"We were contacted by the milkman who heard the car running when making his rounds. We haven't advised Mr. Shaw about any of this, yet."

"Let me take care of that," Reg said, his voice cracking with emotion.

"Are there any other children?" the officer asked.

"Yes, one, a boy named Brian."

The officer assured Reg that no other bodies were found.

"I expect that Brian and his father were absent because of their morning train ride into Paris, where Brian attends school."

"We will be back in touch should we learn more. This is a tragedy of gigantic proportions," the officer said.

Reg headed to the *Tribune* office where he found Seth sitting at his desk reading the morning newspaper.

"Seth, I—"

"My God, man, what's wrong?" Seth said as he stood.

"I . . . I—"

"Out with it, man, whatever it is. It can't be that bad."

Reg took a deep breath and continued.

"Seth, I don't know how to tell you this without . . . Mimi, Rosie, and the girls . . . they're all dead . . . gone."

"WHAT? What're you saying?"

"They're all dead, Seth. Mimi killed herself by leaving the car engine running. The fumes seeped into the bedroom above the garage. Rosie was sleeping with the girls."

Seth pitched forward into Reg's arms and passed out. An office worker administered smelling salts, but Seth fought returning to consciousness. When his eyes opened, they were glazed over with confusion. Finally, he spoke.

"I could sense it, a foreboding, a negative feeling." He thought for a moment. "What about the boy? Does Brian know?" Seth asked.

"No, not yet."

Seth immediately set out for Marymount. Not trusting himself to drive, he asked Reg to join him. The Black Dog was not only present but ripping at Seth's throat. He could hardly speak.

Inside the headmaster's oversized office, Seth provided details. "Before Brian arrives, you should know that he suffers from occasional bouts of depression," he told the headmaster. "I'm concerned he'll break down and maybe even hurt himself."

"Mr. Shaw, we have the means here to provide help for any of our charges who have special needs."

"You mean licensed psychologists?"

"Yes."

Brian arrived and immediately sensed something dire had occurred, seeing his father glassy-eyed and flush.

"Something terrible has happened, hasn't it?" Brian asked.

"Yes son, your—"

Seth couldn't finish, so Reg continued.

"I'm so sorry to have to tell you this, Brian, but your mother and your sisters have died."

Brian's knees buckled; his expression frozen as he flopped into an office chair across from the headmaster's desk.

Reg provided details. The headmaster then spoke.

"Brian, this is a terrible occurrence. We can only wonder why these things happen. Please know that we stand behind you. We offer you any help you might need. Let God in His grace and wisdom be with you. God bless you, boy."

Stunned, Brian remained silent.

Father John traveled to Paris for the memorial service. His eulogy was magnificent, as was the service he conducted at graveside. Because everyone on the staff wished to be present, the *Tribune* closed for the day. Seth was quite moved by the show of support. Afterwards, Father John met with Seth, who had taken a room at the Ritz because he couldn't bear to be in the house where his wife and daughters had died.

"Seth, how are you holding up?"

"Not well."

"Tell me what you're feeling."

"I feel cheated. I shed my ugly skin. Purged away my wicked ways. Brought Christ into my life. Accepted Him as my Lord and Savior. And then this happened. It's the perfect opportunity to kick me in the teeth after concluding that I don't deserve such happiness."

"I can assure you that God doesn't hurt people or punish them. He doesn't zap us to see us squirm. Remember how he saved you at the restaurant. Obviously, He loves you totally and completely."

"Father, that assurance isn't good enough, not when I lose my wife and two of my children."

"I can't hope to fathom what you're now feeling, Seth. There's nothing I can say that can make your pain go away. Even so, don't let your faith slip away."

Father John got up to leave. Seth followed him to the door.

"You know I've been praying for you," he said

Seth nodded.

A week later, Reg asked Seth to meet him for breakfast at the Ritz.

"How is Brian?"

"Doesn't say much, but I know he's bleeding inside," Seth said.

"Seth, I have more news, not entirely good."

"Fire away," Seth mocked. "It can't get any blacker."

"I told you I'd tell you when it became imminent," Reg said.

"You mean the sale of the paper?"

"Yes."

"By God, everything happens at once."

"Word has it that it will happen soon. The Colonel is convinced that there is room for only one newspaper like ours over here. He intends to make an offer to buy the *Paris Herald*. If they don't accept, he intends to offer the *Tribune* to them."

"I can't say it's a surprise. People have been talking about an impending sale since April. How will it affect you?" Seth asked.

"I'm good either way. They'll keep me at the *Tribune*, and they'll hire me at the *Herald*."

"Do you have any idea what will happen to me?" Seth asked.

"I think you're at risk. They're not likely to honor your investment if a new company is formed. They'll be looking to keep only the most experienced among us."

"What do you recommend I do?"

"You've got to go on assignment to a trouble-spot as soon as possible. That way, if the *Herald* takes over, you'll be safe. They're not likely to recall one of their foreign correspondents."

"Where should I go?"

"Ethiopia."

"Ethiopia?"

"Yes, Ethiopia, also known as Abyssinia. Mussolini has designs on that tiny country.

A meeting with Ralph Frantz took place two days later. Seth got right to the point. "Reg tells me that the best way to protect my job with the paper is to go on foreign assignment. He suggested Abyssinia."

"Why Abyssinia?" Ralph asked.

"Mussolini plans to conquer it. Chief, I'll be honest with you. I love this job. It's what has been holding things together for me. The job of foreign correspondent may help me to keep my position, and my sanity."

"I see. You're certainly being direct and honest."

"Thanks."

The Colonel honored Seth's request for reassignment, and Seth immediately made plans for Abyssinia. He assured Brian that Reg and Elain would take good care of him. Seth was delighted to learn only one week later that a buyer for the house had been secured, and that Reg would handle the arrangements.

A short time after Seth's arrival, Italy invaded Abyssinia. Fascinated by the developing events, Brian listened for news on the radio, and waited anxiously for letters from his father that would come once a week. The war Seth described in his letters and newspaper dispatches was ugly. Troops on horseback were slaughtered by Italian tanks and artillery. Poisonous gas, and daylight bombing were used against helpless civilians.

Brian and Reg were driving to Paris together, on Brian's regular commute.

"Uncle Reg, Dad's got to get out of there," Brian said.

"I agree. The Italians are close to capturing Addis Ababa, and that will end it," Reg said.

"Uncle Reg, I've got a bad feeling about this."

"So do I. Read his most recent letter," Reg said.

Dear Reg:

What is happening here is evidence of what can happen when evil takes hold of a good people. The Italians have given us Michelangelo and Leonardo Da Vinci. Then along comes Mussolini with his fascist friends and leaves a blot that can never be wiped away. Brutality has erupted here on a scale that the world has never seen before. These fascists think nothing of bombing undefended cities and gassing unprotected troops. But the worst of it is the genocide. The intellectuals are being rounded up and slaughtered, systematically. Teachers are being eliminated in great numbers. Mussolini has pulled out all the stops. And there is no meaningful opposition. The League of Nations has been too cowardly to act, and Britain and France aren't ready to intervene. Mark my words. Hitler is studying what is happening here with intense interest.

Worst of all, the newspaper has ignored many of my submissions. I suspect that they are reluctant to challenge Mussolini. I deal with the Black Dog every day now. The only time it loosens its grip is when I put myself in danger, and I'm getting closer and closer to the front lines every day. If something happens to me, Brian will be well taken care of, thanks to the trust at the Elgin Bank. As for any impact I've made, it feels like I've written my name in ink on water. Nothing of significance remains.

Sorry to be so negative,
Love,
Seth

"Uncle Reg, he's going to do something desperate, I know it," Brian said. "I feel it."

A telegram came the following week announcing that Seth had been killed by a fascist sniper a few miles outside of Addis Ababa. Ralph Frantz called Reg to report the details.

"He got too far out front. Spotted by a sniper, he was killed instantly. It's almost as though he was challenging the Fates."

CHAPTER SEVENTEEN

Reverend Paul F. Ewald and Father John shared responsibility for the memorial service at Alphonse Church in Chicago. Afterwards, Reg and Brian meet in attorney Duane Negley's Elgin office for the reading of the will. There were no surprises except for three unexpected bequests—Reverend Ewald and Father John each received one million dollars and Reg received twice that amount. In each case, the funds were to be distributed with no strings attached. Overwhelmed, Reg felt his eyes puddling.

"I know my father regarded the attack at Rivoli's as the great turning point in his life. To him, his escape from death was nothing less than a miracle. In fact, his recommitment to Christianity occurred a short time afterward. Still, I'm concerned that he had lost his faith considering the many tragedies he endured."

"Brian, your father has always talked freely with me about his faith," Negley said. "He has never indicated in any of our conversations that he no longer believed. To him, the tragedies were part of a separate curse that had nothing to do with the Black Dog. The curse is the culprit, not God, he once told me. As far as I know, he never wavered in his faith. I'll prove it to you."

Negley took two documents out of his file and handed them to Brian.

"They were included with his last letter, obviously intended for you."

Brian read the poems, written by his dad just weeks before his death:

THE SHADOW BOXER
Are you secure in your faith?
Don't be so sure.
The Shadow Boxer is always there,
lurking unseen in the shadows
ready to cajole any unwary believer
with his hateful pitch—

"The Garden of Eden is a myth.
Mary was no virgin.
Bethlehem wasn't the place
where Jesus was born.
Forget about the stable and the star
and scratch the wise men who supposedly
came from afar.
Jesus was a prophet, nothing more.
There was no resurrection.
Scheming Jews moved the body
with no fear of detection."

Don't be taken in by such blasphemy.
The Shadow Boxer, the Devil's emissary,
isn't someone you can trust.
If you buy into his lies,
there's a good chance
you'll forfeit your place
on the celestial bus.

STUTTER STEPS

Pastor, you say that God created the Universe.
Come on! That myth is for ignorant souls
who don't have a clue.
Since then, we've learned so much—
billions of galaxies, containing billions of stars,
along with bottomless black holes
that are difficult to view,
and planets, so many planets,
many perhaps in galaxies like ours
with planets circling around a single star.
Since we don't even know
where the universe begins or ends,
isn't the concept of a God-created universe
a stretch too far?

Zelda, the gaps in our knowledge
shouldn't cause defeat.
We may be unable to calculate
the total number of stars
or predict when Christ
will return to meet us,
still, isn't it just as easy
to embrace unprovable concepts
as it is to doubt?
Isn't that what Faith is all about?

Pastor, you talk about Faith—
precision, design, science, physics
and mathematics
are what give us faith.
The Faith, that you describe
is only for fools.

Zelda, the Bible tells us
to embrace our Faith with zest,
like little children.
Did you ever watch a young swimmer
standing at the edge of a pool
with his back to the water
and his arms crossed in front?
Looking straight ahead, he falls back,
letting the water embrace him
unconcerned about
what theory of the Universe is best
or the formula for water or the reason it holds him up.
Without looking back, he gives a shout
confident that a safe landing is never in doubt.
Zelda, that's what Faith is all about.

IT KEEPS ON TICKING

About twenty years give or take—`
that's all you've got
with most appliances.
Even a furnace has been known to go,
one year too soon
in the dead of winter
when there's ten feet of snow.
By comparison, how efficient and durable
our circulatory systems seem to be
churning away inside of us.
As part of God's plan, in the average lifetime
the heart beats close to 3 billion times
and for me at age seventy-plus,
it has kept on ticking at a steady pace
well beyond the average span.
Can there be any doubt that this miraculous machine

is a product of God not man?

MIRACLE IN A MIRROR
Pastor, I wonder why the Lord shortchanges us
when it comes to miracles.
If He's as powerful as you say,
why doesn't He regularly show His hand,
to keep the skeptics at bay?

Jeremy, there's no need for a grand show.
Nature's beauty, which is all around us,
gives us the way to go.

Pastor, love of nature is fine,
but for me bushes and trees
aren't proof of the divine.

Jeremy, try looking in a mirror.
Your body is a Testament.
During your gestation period
your crucial parts are Heaven-sent,
all with specified functions—
a bone structure to support your weight,
a rugged cranium to protect your brain,
ligaments and muscles to improve your gait,
pericardia to safeguard your heart,
a thoracic cavity to encase your lungs.
How do you think all of that came to be?

Evolution, genetics, DNA—
Pastor, I'm sure you studied Darwin
in your day.

Jeremy, the Darwin Dodge has been used for many a year.
The miracle of your body is a perfect negation.
Take the labyrinthine structure of your inner ear,
or the vast network of arteries and veins
or the heart that keeps beating year after year,
or the tear ducts in place to help you cry,
or the phenomenal complexity of each eye.
It's a masterpiece of precision
set up especially for your personal glory
and it performs each function right on cue.
Design is the word . . . with the word Divine added in.
End of story.

Brian went on to graduate from Marymount with flying colors and then to Cornell. After graduating with high honors, he attended law school at the University of Pennsylvania and within weeks after graduation enlisted in the Army Air Corps. It wasn't long before he was a pilot flying B-17's in Europe, facing near death experiences. His last flight had been particularly harrowing. He was forced to parachute over enemy territory and would have been captured by the Gestapo but for the bravery of a beautiful young Resistance fighter named Phoebe, who helped him to escape.

Having gone through war at its worst, Brian had difficulty dealing with peace time. Trying to get on with his life, he applied to several large law firms all anxious to hire the war hero. He settled on a Pittsburgh firm that offered him a position of associate with a high salary. Soon Brian was bored by the work. *I've got to get away,* he thought. His plan was to return to Paris first and then decide where to go from there. A senior partner offered little encouragement when Brian asked for a leave of absence, being told that a job might not be waiting for him should he decide to return.

Once in France, Brian sought out Phoebe, the young women in the Resistance who had saved his life. He hoped to find her in her native Brussels.

While sitting alone in a passenger train, the door to his compartment opened with a bang and a large man entered wearing the kind of tweed jacket and camel-hair vest favored by British gentlemen. He also wore a derby and carried an umbrella which seemed to compliment his brush mustache and thick British accent.

"Do you object to company?" the man asked.

"Certainly not."

The man placed a small bag in the overhead compartment and the umbrella on the seat and sat opposite Brian.

"Let me introduce myself. I'm Grayson Straymore."

"I'm Brian Shaw," Brian said, extending his hand.

"You're an American."

"Is it that obvious?"

"I'm afraid so," Straymore said.

Brian looked casual by comparison, wearing gray slacks and a gray woolen sweater over a white shirt, no tie, his blue blazer folded neatly on the seat beside him. He looked powerful and handsome.

"What gave me away?"

"Your accent, and I've got another suspicion."

"What's that?'

"I think you served in the armed forces."

"Right again. You've got to tell me your secret. I signed up with the Army Air Corps after law school and ended up with the Eighth Air Force."

"Served myself, British Intelligence. Spent my time at MI-9 in London, a desk job basically. I'm headed for Brussels. How about you?"

"Same destination," Brian said.

"Where were you stationed during the war?"

"Thorpe Abbots with the 100th Bomber Group."

"Ah yes, the Bloody 100th."

They were referring to Thorpe Abbots Airbase located approximately a hundred miles northeast of London, between Cambridge and Norwich, at a location out of the reach of the German Luftwaffe.

"You are correct."

"And I suspect you flew B-17's."

"Correct again."

Almost immediately Brian felt a camaraderie with this man, and relaxed.

"Are you a married man?" Straymore asked.

"No. I'm on leave from a law firm."

"What brings you to Europe?"

"It's a long story. Do you really want to hear it?"

"Fire away."

The train pulled out of the station with a shudder. Soon, the countryside outside the window began to speed by—a haystack, cattle grazing, fields of corn, then wheat, then corn again. Brian began slowly, describing his decision to enlist in 1941. After basic training as a pilot, he received orders to fly a brand-new B-17 to Thorpe Abbots as a co-pilot. Before each bombing run, he would rub a rabbit's foot hanging above the instrument panel. He did so for each of the twenty odd missions he had flown, always returning home safely.

"During the warmup for one particular flight, I discover that the rabbit's foot is missing. The crew was devastated, but there was no time to go back for it or to find a substitute.

"Over their target in northern Germany, after taking flak the plane wouldn't climb at the normal rate and we had difficulty staying in formation.

"By the time the Nazi fighters came, we were sitting ducks. One by one they swooped down with guns blazing. The first burst killed the pilot."

"Your pilot! Definitely a bad piece of luck," the Brit said

"The attackers shoot up the tail so badly that the plane quickly lost altitude. I held it steady until the crew bailed out, and then followed. I landed hard in a field and snapped my right leg. Seconds later, two farmers ran up and dragged me to a nearby hedgerow after hiding the parachute in a drainage ditch. Then the men fled.

"I found out later that the farmer and his son ran off out of concern for their safety and that of their family. German civilians who assisted American fliers were likely to be shot or hanged.

Straymore nodded.

"I don't think the Nazis would have put me in front of a firing squad, but they sure would've made things uncomfortable for me and I had no desire to sit out the war in a prison camp."

After a few hours of lying in the hedgerow in severe pain, Brian dragged himself to a nearby farmhouse. An elderly man and his wife shared what little food they had and then helped him into a barn nearby. In broken English they told him that a young woman named Phoebe would visit him in the morning. When she arrived, she instructed him that she was with the French Resistance and would personally escort him to a safe house that evening after it got dark.

Brown-haired and brown-eyed with delicate features, Phoebe had disguised herself to look like a young teenager—white stockings rolled at the top, short skirt, hair in a ponytail. Up close, however, she was all woman, beautiful, brilliant, ramrod tough, and in her twenties. She arranged for him to be smuggled by wagon to a safe house outside of Brussels where a doctor visited to set his leg. Once there, she instructed him to remain indoors, avoid windows, talk in whispers, and flush the toilet only once a day. While hiding out, Phoebe and Brian came to know each other well. She told him about the Freedom Line, which was a proven escape route to be used in escorting downed pilots out of France and Belgium, but they would have to wait until his leg was sufficiently healed to make the trip.

"Those of us stationed in London were keenly aware of the Freedom Line," Straymore said, listening intently to Brian's story. It was an escape route for downed airmen that extended from Brussels through France and Spain to Gibraltar."

"British connections in Gibraltar provided me with safe passage to London," Brian added.

"I am very familiar with the woman you speak of," Straymore said. "She was part of the French Resistance. Out of London we did everything in our power to assist her. It took a lot of guts to do what she did. Do you realize that for every airman saved, one of those brave souls in the Resistance perished? If caught, they were brutally tortured and then shot, regardless of gender or age."

"So, she truly risked her life for me," Brian said.

"As did many others. Phoebe became the brains behind the operation," Straymore said.

"You seem to know an awful lot about her," Brian said.

"It was a banner day for us in MI-9 when Phoebe first came forward to assist."

"Did you ever meet her?" Brian asked.

"Never had the pleasure, but she became a legend for all of us at MI-9 just the same—very brave, very brilliant, very resourceful, very beautiful. I think every man she ever met fell in love with her."

"I certainly did, I can tell you that," Brian laughed.

"A fantastic leader, she saved hundreds of airmen. The Gestapo refused to believe that a person so young, especially a woman, could do what she did."

"She was very proud of her ability to speak English," Brian said. "She would get angry when I teased about her bad pronunciations. She would laugh, her face lighting up like a Christmas tree. She was quite charming. I adored her. She didn't hesitate to bring in a physician to set my leg even though she and he were aware of the danger."

"Yes," Straymore added. "During the Occupation, the Gestapo

watched all doctors closely."

"Fortunately, Phoebe checked on me every day while my leg mended. I taught her to play gin, and she ended up beating me regularly. At the end of the first week, we made love. I assured her I would return someday, which is what I'm doing now."

When his leg healed, Phoebe escorted him down the Freedom Line into Spain. From there he traveled on to Gibraltar and eventually to London.

"Got out by the skin of my teeth, thanks to her."

"Did she describe what happened to her after your escape?"

"I'm totally in the dark about that. The one letter I received from her was very cryptic."

"Brian, I've got a confession to make."

"What's that?"

"Our meeting today isn't a chance encounter."

"I was beginning to suspect that."

"Phoebe telephoned me. As an old friend and colleague, she urged me to intercept you and persuade you not to come."

"How were you able to find me?" Brian asked.

"You aren't hard to spot, and I knew when you would be coming."

"Why would she feel the need to discourage me?"

"You probably aren't aware that the Gestapo captured—"

"She was captured?"

"Did they— hurt her?"

"Terribly."

"That's why she wanted me to stop you. You see, she feels that her face is grotesque because of the mutilation. She doesn't want anyone to see her."

"Nonsense—there's always plastic surgery. Doctors today do wonders, and I have plenty of money to pay for whatever is needed."

"Not for her. She wears the mutilation like a badge. In her mind it's retribution for her shame."

"Her shame?"

"Yes, you see, during the pain of torture she provided the names of members of her organization, most of whom were later executed. She feels personally responsible."

"Don't be ridiculous. A person can only stand so much."

"She doesn't see it that way. In her mind, the Germans took her soul when they made her betray her associates. Her only role now, as she sees it, is to live out the balance of her life alone and in disgrace."

"How bad is it?" Brian asked.

"I've not seen the scars myself so I can't tell you from direct knowledge, but from what I hear, it's bad. The bastards broke her jaw, and then they—"

"What? What did they do?"

"They slashed both sides of her face with a razor."

Brian covered his face in his hands. Straymore continued.

"Brian, I know this is painful for you. I'm told she tries to hide the scars behind a plastic mask that she holds in front of her face. As you can probably imagine, the mask is very inadequate."

"I've got to see her., Brian said.

"My job is to dissuade you and, if that doesn't work, prepare you," Straymore said.

"Will you be coming with me?"

"No. I promised her I'd let you come alone if I wasn't able to convince you to turn back."

The train pulled into the Brussels station and the two men shook hands, embraced, and sadly parted on the platform.

"I hope all goes well," Straymore said. "Give her my best. Tell her that she'll always be first on my list."

"I will."

Straymore disappeared into the steam and mist at the end of the platform as Brian flagged down a taxi. Inside, he removed a letter from his breast pocket.

"Driver, please take me to 160 rue Marie-Christine. Do you know where that is?"

"Yes, it's where the streetcar line ends."

A few minutes later the cab stopped in front of several row houses. Brian paid the driver, removed his bag, and rang the doorbell. The door was partially open. A voice from above called out.

"Come up, Brian. Come to the second floor."

He recognized the accent at once. At the top of the stairs, he stopped. Across the room was a figure in a thick white robe worn over heavy pajamas lying barefoot on a chaise. She held a plastic mask in front of her face.

"Phoebe, is that you?"

"Yes Brian, it's good to see you, but don't come any closer. Put your bag in the corner and sit over there."

Brian complied.

"Phoebe, I'm so sorry to—"

"Tell me about yourself."

He filled her in, describing his experiences following his honorable discharge.

"If it hadn't been for you, I'd probably be dead."

Phoebe responded quickly.

"All that happens at another time, in another world. I was young, full of bravado. I never thought that anything bad would happen to me. I convinced myself that, if caught, I could charm my way out of the mess. But, you see, I was a fool, a naïve fool who turned out to be a coward."

"You are no coward. You saved hundreds of lives. You were extremely brave to have done what you did. Do you know who betrayed you?"

"Yes, a traitor named Paul Vallon, the same scum who deceived your crew. He rounded them up and sent them all to the Gestapo. They all ended up in prisoner-of-war camps thanks to him, the worst kind of collaborator. I don't know how many of your crew survived."

"This Vallon, is he still living?"

"No. Two years after the war ended, he had a sudden accident. It took a while to uncover his treachery and his whereabouts, but my compatriots had long memories. However, his death didn't appease my own sense of guilt."

"Given enough pain, each of us has a breaking point, Phoebe."

"Have you ever heard of Jean Moulin?" she asked.

"Yes, of course, the famous French Resistance fighter."

"Yes, a great hero. Captured by the Gestapo, he never broke. Despite torture, he refused to give names. He acted the way I should have acted."

She continued to hold the mask in front of her face, her voice wavering.

"Moulin became a symbol for me—my opposite."

"Phoebe, I know a little about Moulin, and I can tell you that your assumptions about him are incorrect. To keep him a hero, the French government has hidden the truth. Are you sure you want me to continue?" he asked.

"Yes, but don't tell me that Moulin was a collaborator. I couldn't bear to hear it."

"He wasn't a collaborator, Phoebe. Am I correct that you don't know the exact details about his death?"

"I know only that he died a hero."

"Phoebe, Jean Moulin jumped headfirst into a well located on Gestapo property."

"You mean he—?"

"Yes, he committed suicide before they could torture him."

"How do you know these things?"

"Because of you, after I left the Army, I tried to learn as much about the French Resistance as I could. Moulin's name came up repeatedly. He was a brave man, but he knew his limitations. He ended his life because he feared he might cave under torture."

Phoebe began to sob, tears streaming.

Brian moved toward her. Sitting on the edge of the chaise, he gently removed the mask from her hand and was relieved to see that her wounds weren't as severe as he imagined.

In time, Phoebe gave Brian the complete story. She had been arrested in 1943 during a return trip to Brussels after escorting yet another flier successfully down the Freedom Line. She was to meet a contact in a café but was captured by two Gestapo agents who brought her to meet their colonel.

"Phoebe, my name is Colonel Kieffer. You don't need to be afraid of me. I'm known for my easy ways in cases where the subject cooperates. I always try to obtain the necessary information without violence."

His spoke French with a thick German accent. He stopped talking long enough to show his teeth, like some perfidious reptile. "If a peaceful approach doesn't work, then I send my subjects to Fresnes Prison where the methods are somewhat more severe."

He stood facing her, taken by her beauty.

"We've known about you and your Freedom Line for some time. We waited to make our move until the time was right. By the way, Emil Gunther, the man you are supposed to meet, is dead after taking a cyanide pill."

"I don't know what you're talking about. You have no reason to hold me."

"Ah but we do, Phoebe, and you know we do."

"Considering what we now know, it makes no sense for you to withhold information. If you don't cooperate, you'll put yourself in jeopardy. I'll give you one hour to identify your comrades. If you refuse, you'll be sent to Fresnes."

"Go fuck yourself."

"Suit yourself. You should know, however, that the ugly brutes at Fresnes are prepared to make things very unpleasant for you."

"Go fuck yourself."

"It's late today. I'll check with you in the morning."

The next morning a matron in uniform led Phoebe from her cell to a small conference room beside Kieffer's office.

"The Colonel has instructed me to leave a sheet of paper and pencil on this table so that you can write down the names he has requested. Meantime, you will remain here with the door locked."

"You can kiss my ass."

"He will return in one hour. If you have not responded, you will learn about Fresnes firsthand, and you will not like what you learn."

"How do you expect me to write with these on?" Phoebe asked as she holds up her handcuffs.

"I'm sure you'll find a way."

When the woman slammed the door, Phoebe could hear the lock turning.

One day later, Phoebe, still shackled, stood terrified in a room at Fresnes Prison, a room splotched with blood on the walls and floor. A type of tub filled with water stood in one corner, and in the other, there was a bloodstained mattress. With a crash, the large metal door at the far end of the room opened and a man entered. Naked to the waist, he wore black boots and grey jodhpurs held up by black suspenders. When he leaned in close, she could smell his body odor and foul breath. He was accompanied by a matron in a nurse's uniform, and he spoke to her in German.

"Help me tie her down," he said as Phoebe was strapped naked to a long table located in front of the tub of water.

"That's all," he said, and the matron left the room.

When he tilted the table Phoebe's head was plunged under the water. At just the last moment when her lungs were about to explode, he brought her back up. Each time he asked for the information that Kieffer had been requesting, and each time she spit water in his face. After three submersions there was no change.

"Very good. Most of my charges spill their guts after one plunge. Because of your toughness, I'm forced to become a bit more inventive. I think it's time to work on your facial features. You're so beautiful. It will be such a shame."

Still clamped to the board, she felt pliers in her mouth. A twisting motion produced a crunching sound as her jaw fractured.

"You bastard!"

"Phoebe girl, this is just the beginning. Won't you tell me what we want to know so that we won't have to ruin your face?"

Phoebe said nothing and watched as the grotesque man picked up a straight razor and began slashing both sides of her face.

"Stop! Stop! for God's sake stop! I'll give you what you want."

And she did.

On a piece of paper that had been left on one of the benches, she wrote the names and addresses of three colleagues. Phoebe was then sent to a prison doctor who treated her wounds only superficially and then sent her back to her cell, where she sat racked with guilt and shame. *They will be executed and it's because of my cowardice.* Deep depression soon followed.

Later, one of the guards told her that the next move would probably be to Dachau, and the thought of being confined in such a place added to her misery. Two days later Phoebe was forced into a boxcar with several other prisoners, the stench unbearable. She assumed that most of the people in the car were Jews destined along with her to die. Instead, she was spared and freed when the Allies liberated the camp. Before the Allies hanged him, Colonel Kieffer admitted that he had entered a special-order sparing Phoebe's life. When pressed for a reason, he admitted that she reminded him of a daughter. According to him, the resemblance was uncanny.

In Brussels, it wasn't long after his arrival that Brian asked Phoebe to marry him. As much as she loved him, Phoebe hesitated. *He doesn't love me. He feels sorry for me, that's all.* Eventually, Brian wore her down. No friends or family attended the ceremony in Brussels. Two weeks after the wedding, they booked passage on a ship to the states and settled into a large house outside of Chicago. Week after week she endured the pain of several operations. After six months it came down to a final unveiling. A nurse held a large mirror in front of Phoebe as the doctor removed the bandages. Phoebe gasped.

"Phoebe, it's miraculous," Brian said. "You look like you did when I first met you."

She knew he was lying but went along.

"It's as good as they could do," she said.

"Give it time, darling, give it time."

CHAPTER EIGHTEEN

Brian's legal career plummeted after he lost one lawsuit after another. At crucial moments, his mind would go blank, causing him to sputter and crash in front of judges, juries, and witnesses. Two law firms fired him, pushing Brian into depression and early retirement. Still wealthy from his inheritance, Brian and Phoebe lived very comfortably, but without much sense of purpose or happiness.

Stephen, their only child, was born late in their marriage, and was their joy. But he began to show signs early on of social dysfunction, as his father and grandfather had before him. By the summer of 1969, at eighteen years of age, Stephen was having difficulty getting along with his father. Stephen was aware that his father had suffered several setbacks over the years that had caused his persistent depressions and erratic moods, a condition his father called the Black Dog. Even though his father's erratic personality was thus explained, the explanation didn't help to eradicate the tension between them. Fortunately, Stephen was close to his mother, Phoebe, who was always willing to intercede if the father-son interplay became impossible. When Stephen first learned of a summer position with a construction company in California, he made the mistake of going to his father first to discuss the opportunity. His father was adamant.

"I don't want you driving out there by yourself," he said. "The world is a crazy place, Stephen, especially in California."

"It's only for the summer," Stephen said.

"I don't care."

"Dad, I'm eighteen years old and I can take care of myself. Nothing bad is going to happen to me."

"You're not going."

Only after his mother intervened did Brian come around. She reminded Brian that Barney Foster, the youth minister at the church, would accompany Stephen on the trip. When Barney became sick at the last moment and cancelled, Stephen never told his parents and went on the trip. *When Dad learns about Barney's change of plans, I'll be well on my way. There will be no way to reach me.*

The drive west in his father's blue Thunderbird was boring and hot, especially with the top down. When Stephen saw a sign promising Los Angeles in twenty miles, he was overjoyed. After one or two wrong turns he entered a small town and noticed a tattoo parlor. He abruptly turned into the gravel lot. *Dad will have a shitfit if I get a tattoo, which is a very good reason to get one.*

This tattoo parlor's walls were covered with mounted animal heads plus various types of fishing rods and firearms. In an open area up front, a tattoo artist was at work on the posterior of a young woman, who looked over her shoulder.

"We heard your grand entrance."

She was certainly attractive, but not gorgeous by any means. She had a look of innocence about her.

"What's the matter, cowboy, cat got your tongue? Don't you want to talk to Matty and me?" the girl said

The needle buzzed on girl's milk-white posterior, a towel hiding her private parts. The tattoo artist looked like a vagrant, displaying a filthy T-shirt with no sleeves over dirty jeans and bare feet, wallet in his back pocket attached to his belt by a chain. On his arms and legs were hundreds of tattoos.

"Sure, I do," Stephen finally replied. "What do they call you?" he asked the girl getting the tattoo.

"I'm Dotty and this here is Matty," she said of the guy working the needles. "Listen, cowboy, if it shakes you up to see my sweet ass, Matty and me can go into the back room."

"No, not at all. On the contrary, your behind is the nicest thing I've seen this morning."

"Well, thank you, cowboy."

Matty continued his work without smiling or looking up. For the next half-hour there was little conversation. At last, Matty raised his hands with a flourish.

"There, it's done, a masterpiece."

"Cowboy, what do you think?" Dotty asked after removing the towel and revealing her pubic hair. Stephen became aroused. Still bent over, Dotty looked up at him, smiling.

"Looks pre . . . pretty good to me," Stephen stuttered.

The tattoo was like nothing he'd ever seen before. Dark, it contrasted greatly with Dotty's fair skin, looking like a black handprint on a white-marble wall. The tattoo's animal head snarled outward, accentuated by bloody fangs.

"What's your name?" Dotty asked.

"Stephen."

"I like *cowboy* better. Would you be willing to take me home, Cowboy?"

The more Stephen studied her, the more attractive she appeared.

"Before we run off together, I want to get a tattoo. Can you wait?"

"Looks like you're worth waiting for, Cowboy."

Stephen selected a small panther to be displayed on his left soldier. "That tattoo looks small on your shoulder," Dotty said.

"How do you mean?"

"You've got big shoulders. You know what they say, big shoulders, big dick," she laughed.

Embarrassed, Stephen looked away. No woman had ever spoken to him like that before. Dotty snickered.

"Oh, look, Matty, the pretty cowboy is embarrassed. I didn't mean to shock you. Whether your equipment is large or small doesn't much matter to me. I've had experience with all sizes—haven't I, Matty?"

"I guess you could say that" Matty grunted.

Looking at the long legs and the tight-fitting blue jean shorts, Stephen realized his fascination with this young woman had turned to lust. At the same time something deep inside cautioned him to be wary but lust overruled his caution. From the moment she sat beside him on the front seat, her demeanor changed. Inside the tattoo parlor she was flippant and carefree; in the car she was serious and somber.

"Where do you live," he asked.

"The Spahn Ranch, with several other girls. All runaways, like me. The East Coast was boring and my stepfather . . . well, you know."

Stephen pulled over to the side of the road to put the top up so he could better hear what she was saying.

A man named Charlie had taken Dotty in, along with several other homeless girls. She had met Charlie at a bus terminal.

"He considers himself to be a prophet, a wizard, and a seer all combined into one package. If he has a last name, I don't know what it is."

"Sounds like a real character."

"He terrifies me," she said.

"How so?"

"You'd have to look at him to understand."

"You mean he's sinister looking?"

"That's an understatement. He's evil incarnate, with the wildest yellow eyes you ever saw, I mean, the wildest. The Devil's eyes—I swear there's nothing he won't do. I hear noises at night."

"What kind of noises?"

"One night I heard a man screaming, down by the creek, behind the trailer. It was horrible. I'm sleeping in a room with two other girls.

They deny hearing it, but they are brainwashed. There's no way they don't hear it. The screams are blood-curdling."

"Why don't you get out of there?"

"I'm afraid to leave. I'm afraid he'll kill me if I try to go. He's that crazy and he's got spies everywhere. Matty's one of them. I wouldn't get five feet without serious help. I know that much."

"Why the tattoo?"

"It's his brand. Every girl is forced to get one after one year."

"What does it mean?"

"Charlie is a devil worshiper, among other things. Supposedly, he gets his power from Satan. The tattoo is to confirm that we're part of his evil family. We are disciples from that point on, part of his cult. Until now, I've been excluded from the rituals, but I watch the reaction of other girls who've been allowed to participate."

"How so?"

"They haven't told me directly, but when they return to the sleeping quarters, I can see the horror reflected on their faces, and after the rituals, I see bones on the ground, tiny bones, human bones."

"Have the other girls told you anything?"

"No, no details. Only that the rituals are bizarre, incredible, even outrageous. Inside the trailer, I can hear the incantations, and I can see the huge fire on the other side of the trees."

"But the women won't talk?"

"All they can say is that they've sworn in blood to remain silent. In my view, they're afraid, I mean *petrified*, even the ones who are crazy on dope."

She told Stephen that Charlie kept many of the girls under his control with the help of drugs, usually LSD. The only way Dotty had kept her sanity, she said, was by tossing the drugs away after pretending to swallow them. She was convinced that Charlie was fully aware of her deception but had put up with it because she was so good in bed.

"I'm deathly afraid of him. One misstep and I know he'll kill me.

He's constantly telling me that he loves me best of all, and that sex with the other girls means nothing, but even if that were true, which I doubt, that won't stop him from killing me. He goes both ways. He won't miss me or any other girl for long."

"How do you know he's a killer?"

"People keep disappearing. They'll wander into our camp, eat with us for a couple of days, then one morning they're no longer here, and Charlie ends up selling the person's gear. I've heard the screams at night."

Stephen stared straight ahead, silently.

"What about going to the police?"

"There's no concrete evidence. All I would do is tip my hand with Charlie, then he'd kill me."

Stephen understood why she asked him for the ride. He reached for the cigarettes in his breast pocket, offering one to her, which she refused.

"There's something else," she said.

"What's that?"

"There's something big coming down."

Stephen was almost afraid to ask.

"What do you mean by *something big*?"

"I think they're planning what Charlie calls a rampage. Charlie is always talking about starting a race war. I think he's planning to attack in a way that will cause the public to blame the Blacks."

"How do you know this?"

"Tex has been meeting with him more than usual. Tex is crazy-wild, the type of person who will gut-stick you while smiling in your face. They've been having long conferences. As crazy as Charlie is, Tex is worse, much worse, let me tell you."

"You're hitting me with a lot all at once."

They were still sitting at the side of the road.

"You've got to help me get out of here," Dotty said. "With me in your car, we can point the front grille toward the East Coast and drive. I'll do anything you want if you take me out of here—anything."

"We'd better stop some place," he said. "So we can talk this over while getting something to eat. If I'm going to help you, I've got to make a few phone calls."

They drove off.

"What about your parents?" he asked.

"Both are dead."

"I'm sorry."

"There's an inn about five miles up the road. I think they're still serving food. Why don't we stop there?" she said.

Stephen's lust had faded to fear. *I've got to get out of here,* he thought. *I'm no hero. What if we've been followed?* His car, a blue T-Bird, wasn't exactly nondescript. *What if Matty has tipped off Charlie—or Tex?* He thought of Matty's toothless maw wagging into a telephone with Charlie on the other end.

When they stopped for lunch, Stephen hid the car behind the restaurant. They sat in one of the booths toward the back so they wouldn't be seen. After eating, Stephen cleared his throat, nervously.

"I'm thinking you can ask for police protection. It's certainly worth a try."

"It's too late . . . look—"

He turned and saw two men approaching, both unshaven and wearing dirty white T-shirts, filthy jeans, and motorcycle boots. The one on the left was much shorter and had eyes that seemed to give off a yellow luminescence. *It must be Charlie. I'm a dead duck.* Stephen felt the man's eyes boring into him as the two approached.

"Charlie, Tex—how they hangin?" Dotty greeted. "Meet Stephen. Stephen, meet Tex and Charlie."

"Hello," Stephen said.

No response.

"Why don't you guys sit down and join us?" Dotty suggested.

Charlie sat on the far side of the booth next to Dotty, Tex next to Stephen.

"Let's just cut the bullshit," Charlie said.

Even from the other side of the booth, Stephen could smell Charlie's bad breath as he leaned out over the table to speak through a mouth that looked like a burned-out furnace.

"Now, Charlie, whatever do you mean?" Dotty teased.

She's got guts. Here I am about to shit my pants and she's putting them on.

"You know exactly what I mean, bitch. You were supposed to wait at the parlor until I came back for you."

"You were late as usual," she said. "And this good man here offered me a ride."

"Why yes, I—"

"Listen, fuck-nuts, you'll keep your damn trap shut if you know what's good for you."

Stephen's voice trembled. "Fuck-nuts? There's no need for that kind of language, especially in front of this lady, I—"

"You say one more word and Tex here will stick you. This bitch ain't no lady," said Charlie, his eyes on fire. "Let me see your driver's license." Stephen removed it and Tex snatched it from his hand then disappeared. Ten minutes later he returned.

"He checks out," Tex said. "He's a nobody from Chicago—came out here for work. There's no connection with the police at all. His father was some kind of a lawyer, but not a criminal one."

"Well, fuck-nuts, it looks like you were just in the wrong place at the wrong time," Charlie said.

Tex rode with Stephen in his car and Dotty rode with Charlie. When they arrived at the Spahn Ranch, they locked Stephen in a trailer. The ranch was actually a movie set that had gone to seed. The buildings were ramshackle. Debris and broken glass and decay lay everywhere. Passing it on the road, a tourist might well think that the property had been condemned before being turned into a dump. The rusted auto wrecks close to the road had a look of permanence, one car with no engine, the other with no undercarriage or doors, and both up on blocks. Through the barred window of the trailer Stephen saw that daylight was fading fast, a possible indication that Tex or Charlie would be coming soon. At that moment he heard someone fumbling with the lock on the trailer door and saw Tex put his head through the opening.

"Charlie wants you . . . now."

This is it. This is when I die.

Stephen walked slowly beside Tex into the main facility, which was as run down as all the other buildings.

"Sit there and don't move," Tex growled.

Charlie arrived minutes later wearing a black shirt, black jeans, and black boots. He had showered, shaved, and combed his hair. Around his neck was a pendant showing the same ugly face that Stephen had seen on Dotty's posterior. Stephen stared with fear at the pendant as Charlie sat, facing him.

"I've been trying to think of what to do with you," Charlie said.

The hypnotic yellow eyes were now staring directly at Stephen who responded with a shaky voice.

"I know that you could kill me if you wanted to. Please don't. My father and mother would be very upset."

Charlie guffawed like a hyena.

"They won't be half as uncomfortable as you'll be if I turn you over to Tex."

"I'm only eighteen. I was just passing through and wanted a tattoo. The lady asked me for a ride."

"Stranger, you seem innocent enough and like a nice kid, maybe a little dumb, but nice. I don't want to kill you, but I must make sure you don't go to the police."

"I don't even like the police. They've never done anything for me. In fact, they once took my driving privileges away for an entire month."

"Stranger, you're a rare one. I could come to like you, but we gotta a problem. Sure as fuck, Dotty spilled her guts to you about me, Tex, and this ranch. I've got a lot of people counting on me. Some of them want to see you dead."

"My mother and father have big bucks," Stephen said. "I'm sure they'd be willing to pay a ransom if you let me go."

"I'll tell you what I'll do. I'll let you go, but if you say anything to the police about what you've seen out here, I'll kill Dotty. I won't even let Tex do it. I'll do it myself. You don't want that to happen, do you?"

"No, sir."

"And I want ten grand from your family sent to me as soon as you get home, or you'll sign her death warrant. Understood?"

"Yes, sir."

"Here's where to send it."

Charlie handed him a piece of paper with an address. Still, he felt his life might be in jeopardy, that he would be killed. Later, inside his car, he expected Tex to spring up from the back seat and stick him. He could almost feel the blade across his throat. He stomped the accelerator.

"WHOOOOEEEEEEEE," he yelled at the top of his lungs.

Instead of reporting for work with the construction company, he drove straight home to Illinois, without stopping except for gas and food. Once home, he told his father the entire story, but Brian refused to send the money even after admitting that ten thousand dollars was pittance. Nor did Brian let Stephen go to the police.

"It would be embarrassing for the family."

When the world learned of the Manson murders, Stephen was wracked by depression. He remained in his room refusing food and visitors. Finally, his father demanded entry.

"You shouldn't beat yourself up over this," Brian said. "Crazy people do crazy things. You certainly didn't make them that way."

Stephen remained silent.

"Besides, in my view Roman Polanski, Sharon Tate's husband, brought the evil on himself by directing *Rosemary's Baby*, a movie about the Devil. In my view, anyone—especially Polanski—who tries to make a profit from that sort of thing brings negative karma on himself. In his case, he brought tragedy down on several people including his wife and child."

Stephen erupted. "You can't be serious. It's just as easy to say that we brought the murders on ourselves when we failed to go to the police or send money."

"That's absurd," Brian said.

When Dotty's face didn't appear in any of the news accounts after the cult was exposed, Stephen felt even worse. *Charlie murdered her. It's my fault.*

As Stephen expected, his father insisted that he remove the tattoo. When the painful procedure was completed, there was nothing left in its place but an ugly scar, a permanent reminder of his near deadly mishap. Haunted by Dotty's death, Stephen became a depressive recluse.

CHAPTER NINETEEN

I n early February 1982, Phoebe and Brian were traveling by car to Stephen's ordination at First Trinity Church in Elgin. Heavy snow from the night before had been ploughed, but the streets were slick and icy from an early rain. Brian drove gingerly.

"Don't get me wrong, Phoebe. I'm proud of him, real proud of him—real proud," he said while carefully navigating. "I just never thought that a child of mine would ever end up in the ministry, that's all."

"I think part of the impetus comes from his guilt over the disappearance of that young woman in California. He has had the local police investigate it, but they've discovered nothing except to confirm that she has disappeared without a trace," Phoebe said.

"It's the damned family curse," Brian said.

"That's ridiculous. You still believe that generations of this family are cursed because of that Soapy character?"

"Yes, I do. And I worry about how it will affect Stephen and his ministry."

Brian stopped for a traffic light.

"Well, at least we'll get our spiritual inspiration from somebody in the family we both know and love," he said.

She smiled. "In your case he'll need all the help he can—"

At that moment, a truck, coming in the opposite direction at a high rate of speed hit an ice patch and skidded out of control, smashing into the passenger side of Brian's car. Phoebe's injuries were so severe that she died that evening in the hospital.

Stephen came as soon as he got the news. Fortunately, his father was only bruised.

"I'm so sorry, Dad."

His father could hardly speak. "It's so sudden. One minute . . . one minute she's alive talking to me, and the next she's—"

"Don't try to talk, Dad. It's too much for you right now."

"I can't believe that God would do this to me."

"God didn't do this, Dad. The other driver did, and the ice, and the truck. It was an accident, a terrible accident pure and simple."

"I wish I could believe that. This family has always been cursed. Think about Rosie and those two little girls, or my father's death in Abyssinia, or the murder of my grandparents in Elgin. The curse has always been with us."

Brian avoided church for the rest of his life. Even Stephen's presence in the pulpit didn't weaken his resolve. In later years, Stephen agreed to share a duplex with his father who had purchased the entire building. Stephen by then had married Stephanie Bowers. Because of Brian's concern about passing on the bipolar curse to family members, he was relieved to learn that Stephanie couldn't have children. Still, his own mental health deteriorated as he for years mourned the loss of his wife.

Stephen remained convinced that although his father was somewhat eccentric, he was harmless enough overall. Stephanie, however, wasn't so sure.

"You remember the last dinner party we had?" she asked.

"I do, but keep in mind that was very soon after Phoebe's death."

"He made a scene, disrupted the entire party."

"Yes, he did, but it won't happen again. I've talked to him."

"I'm not convinced, not at all. But for the fact that it's his birthday, I wouldn't have invited him at all."

"Now, Steph—"

"Well, I wouldn't have."

Brian arrived for the dinner party looking handsome in a blue blazer, red tie, and khakis, presenting himself as a perfect gentleman. When the Willows arrived, he stood up immediately and took Connie Willow's hand while reciting a mantra about his delight at seeing her. Al Willow, her husband, was headmaster of a local prep school.

"Mrs. Willow. I'm pleased to meet you at last. I've heard so much about you."

"Why, Brian, the feeling is mutual, and please call me Connie."

Connie Willow was thin and quite beautiful. Al Willow, fat and ugly, didn't deserve her in Brian's view. Brian estimated a ten-year difference in ages, which put Connie in her late thirties.

By the time Bill and Thelma Thomas arrived, Brian had finished his second southern comfort Manhattan and was mixing himself a third. Even so, he didn't appear to be showing his liquor. He was as gracious with Thelma and Bill as he had been with the Willows.

Bill Thomas wore a red flannel shirt tucked into a pair of grey corduroys; a choice that made Brian feel overdressed. Thelma, in her sixties, might once have been considered attractive, but that time had long since passed. She was now overweight and wrinkled and devoted to women's social causes.

After some discussion in the living room over drinks, everyone adjourned to the dining room. When all were seated and Stephen delivered the blessing, he began to serve an impressive rack of lamb. After desert, Connie asked Thelma about her efforts on behalf of the National Organization for Women.

"It's frustrating for us because there continues to be a disparity in compensation levels between men and women," she said.

Brian had a ready comment.

"I'll tell you what I think. I think there should be a disparity.

Problems begin to occur when women come out of the kitchen into the workplace. They're too emotional to offer anything of value, and they band together to get their way, a tactic that disrupts the office."

"Brian, you can't be serious," Stephanie said. She noticed that he had poured himself yet another drink.

"I'm dead serious, in fact, I'll go one step further. I don't think women should have been given the vote in the first place. Think about it, most of our problems domestically came about after they got it."

"Now, Dad, I know you're putting these ladies on and—"

"Bullshit! I'm telling it like it is, that's all. The women in their infinite wisdom gave us Prohibition. The nation is still reeling from that wonderful failure."

"You're showing your ignorance now," Thelma scolded. "The Volstead Act was passed in October of 1919 and went into effect in January of 1920 before women's suffrage ever became—"

"The timing isn't important. We all know that the decision to legislate morality by way of Prohibition was a female concept. Remember Carrie Nation and her axe, not to mention the Women's Christian Temperance Union founded in 1874."

"Brian, you're starting to get to me if that's what you're trying to do," Thelma said.

"You're getting to *me* as well," Connie added.

"Let's change the subject," Stephanie said.

"No way! I haven't even touched on the most telling female disaster—abortion rights."

Thelma stood.

"Steph, I want to thank you for a wonderful dinner, but Bill and I must be going."

"Al and I will join you. It's past our bedtime as well," Connie said

"There, you see. When discussions get serious, you women always run for the exits," Brian mocked.

Stephanie and Stephen sat at the breakfast table the following morning. Both were in robes with coffee poured.

"How could he have done it? How could he have said what he did? He has ruined yet another dinner party."

"Stef, I know he's losing it, but he's still my father."

"He may be your father but he's not attending any social functions in this house ever again."

"What would you have me do?"

"Perhaps things would have been different if your father had continued taking his bipolar meds."

"You can't take the medication like that with alcohol, and he isn't willing to give up alcohol," Stephen said.

"What if he kills someone with his car?"

"Get serious! He's not going to do that, at least I don't think he will."

"Well, you can't say he didn't have his facts straight," she said.

They both laughed.

"A penny for your thoughts," she said.

"I bet he had a few choice things to say about abortion rights."

They both laughed again.

CHAPTER TWENTY

A few years later Brian died in bed alone and his funeral service was lightly attended.

"I know he was a pain, Steph, but it wasn't his fault," Stephen said of his father.

"He knew what he was doing," Stephanie said.

"His bipolar condition is what changed him," he said.

"The booze changed him," she retorted.

"And he couldn't stop drinking even when it meant that he had to deep six his meds," he said.

"And that's an excuse? I'm expected to overlook his antics because of his alcoholism. Do you know how many times he badgered me about not having children? No matter how many times I told him I was sterile, he wouldn't stop. He would answer that I could have surgery, that we could adopt . . . on and on he kept at it."

"Look, the poor man is deceased. Let's let him rest in peace. I'll change the subject. I need you to critique Sunday's sermon."

Citing appropriate Bible verses, he presented the idea that each one of us has been blessed through God's grace with a soul.

"Steph, if that is the case, how can there be so much evil in the world? At this point I use an analogy. I propose that the soul is like the fire inside a furnace. When we open the furnace door, we can see the fire burning freely. I argue that this condition, this fire, is inside all of us and that it burns perpetually. If so, why doesn't it prevail in all cases to prevent the encroachment of evil?" he asked.

"Because we have free will," she said.

"Correct, but how does free will make a difference? In the analogy, the fire of the soul keeps burning. We know from scripture that once it is inside of us, the fire never goes out. How can that be? Wouldn't that mean that the fruits of the spirit—love, joy, peace, patience, goodness, gentleness, and all the rest—would prevail? Thanks to the Holy Spirit aren't the fruits lodged in our soul? If each of us has a soul, why isn't the world overflowing with God's goodness and grace?"

"I still say free will makes the difference. A single bucket of water is all that is needed to stifle the good effects of the soul, using your analogy," she said.

"Ah, but the fire cannot be quenched. It's a permanent feature burning inside of us, so to speak," he said.

"Okay, what's the answer?"

"Imagine an opening in the furnace door which permits you to see what's going on inside," he said.

"Okay."

"Now imagine a metal grate over the opening that opens and closes the same way our Venetian blinds operate. Free will permits us to close the grate completely, or partially. If our view is obscured or blocked entirely, the power of the soul is eliminated entirely . . . what do you think?"

"Too gimmicky," she laughed.

"I'm going with the analogy anyway. It may not produce a *great* sermon but it's too late to come up with a new one," he laughed.

"I see the pun. Now let me ask you something," she said.

"Fire away."

"We know that the genetic transfer of a bipolar condition can take place, thanks to Soapy Smith. It lodged inside Seth, and it lodged inside Brian as well. We can determine that by following their antics. Brian's symptoms caused him to do strange things at dinner parties.

That being the case, why hasn't the bipolar *curse*, if you want to call it that, affected you. You are Brian's only son?" she asked.

"Maybe it has," he answered. "I experienced some pretty low times after I returned from California and recognized that the young women I met there was probably murdered. I think my depression might have pushed me into the ministry."

"Bad things bring everyone down, but you're rarely depressed, and I've never seen you in a manic state. On top of that, your therapist has opined that you are not bipolar," she said.

"We can thank God for that and for the fact that there hasn't been a tragedy in our family for years," he said.

"No there hasn't. Tragedy would have struck us by now if it was going to strike at all. And the bipolar stain won't ever reach our children because we can't have children. Insofar as this part of the family is concerned, the curse—both curses—are dead."

"Praise the Lord," he said.

CHAPTER TWENTY-ONE

I t was time for the annual church pageant. From past pageants, the congregation was aware of Pastor Stephen's theatrical skills. Every year church members insisted that he do his Mark Twain impression. Stephen told Stephanie that he hated the idea of doing it again but didn't see how to avoid it.

"They're gluttons for punishment, that's for sure," she said laughing.

And so, in the footsteps of Hal Holbrook, he donned his costume, the same he used in all prior years—linen suit, tie, vest, shirt, and shoes, all white, that had been hanging in the closet for twelve months. Next, he searched through the lowest drawer in the bureau until he found the shaggy wig, which, while in place, transformed his hair into what looked like a dandelion gone to seed, a look compounded by the brush mustache. In the changing room behind the church auditorium, Stephanie helped him dress. Just before Stephen went out on the stage, she kissed him, and he moved ahead feeling weak at the knees, unsure whether it was a reaction to her kiss or to the thunderous applause waiting for him. He gave a few introductory comments and then got right to it.

"Rarely is a man fortunate enough to marry the woman of his dreams, but that's exactly what happened to me. To my total surprise, Olivia Langdon accepts my proposal, and on February 2, 1870, we are married at her parents' home in Elmira, New York. Eventually, we rent a house pending the completion of our dream home in Nook Farm near Hartford, Connecticut. I doubt many of you ever heard of Nook Farm, which is not surprising since Nook Farm is a tiny neighborhood you'd miss if you weren't looking for it. Private and rustic, upscale and bucolic, it was the perfect spot for us. When the house was built in 1874, the architect advises Livy and me that the style we have chosen is High Victorian Gothic. As it turns out, his brand of High Victorian Gothic is flexible enough to incorporate the shape of a pilot house giving the house from the front the look of a riverboat. The architect never forgives Livy and me for insisting on that added feature."

Stephen paused to acknowledge the laughter as he poured water into a glass from a nearby pitcher. The audience watched his Adam's apple bob up and down as he swallowed. He harrumphed once or twice in a way that made his white mustache flutter, then continued.

"Some of you may have heard about my piloting experiences on the 'Big Muddy. If so, you may also be aware that *Life on the Mississippi* is my personal account of those experiences. If you haven't purchased the book, please do so. I need the cash. The book describes an incident that happens in 1858 when the boiler on the riverboat Pennsylvania explodes. That tragedy had a special interest for me because my younger brother Henry is on board at the time. Witnesses say he is safely out of danger but swims back to rescue others. That's when the second boiler blows scalding anyone in the water at the time."

Stephen shook his white mane as if fighting back tears.

"Henry's passing is a crushing blow. I blame myself for it. I should have been there. I'm certain I could have saved him. Truth is, on the trip downriver the head pilot kicked me off the Pennsylvania in New Orleans for fighting. I was assigned to another vessel. Because of my hotheadedness, I'm not on the Pennsylvania when the explosion occurs.

"Have you ever gone somewhere and had the feeling that you'd been there before? They call it *déjà vu*. Well, that's what happens to me during the *Pennsylvania* tragedy. I get there in time to find Henry on a hospital bed barely alive. He dies two days later. Dressed in some of my clothes, he is laid out in an open metal casket with a bouquet of roses on his chest, all white except for a single red one. Trouble is, I'd seen all of it before. I mean all of it—the replacement clothes, the metal casket, the wreath with the single red rose—all of it comes to me previously in a dream. In the past I scoff when people tell me they are psychic. Now, I'm a believer.

"Oh, don't get me wrong. My journeys on the river offer wonderful experiences as well. There is nothing more glorious than a sunrise or a sunset on the Big Muddy, or the peace and solitude it offers on summer nights under a full moon. In spring, the air near shore is always sweet and thick with the scent of magnolias or gardenias or Carolina jasmine. All of that being the case, a lot of people ask me why I ever left the river. There is a simple answer: The damn Yankees closed it down. [Laughter]

"I hear you laughing, but it wasn't funny then. The Yankee blockade in 1861 puts me out of business. Thanks to the Union navy, my position as a river pilot is totally pulverized. Out of work as I was, I'm pressed to find a new occupation. One thing is certain. I'm not much interested in becoming a Confederate soldier. My experience in the militia teaches me that army life could be a bit unpleasant. One afternoon, an over-exuberant Yankee took a potshot at me. That Yankee helped me learn that being a target in an armed conflict isn't as great as everyone let's on. [Laughter]

"Thus persuaded, I travel west with my brother Orion, and it is there I met the jumping frog that played such an important role in establishing my writing career. I won't bore you with the details, except to point out that a jumping frog loaded down with buckshot loses all bets. [Laughter]

"Tragedy comes early in our marriage when our first-born son, Samuel Langdon Clemens, dies at the age of two. The doctor opines that he dies of diphtheria, but I've always maintained he dies because of my neglect. You see, I let his blanket slip away from his little body during a winter carriage ride. Truth is, instead of paying attention to my son, I'm in one of my mental funks that causes me to miss the poor child's shivering until we arrive back home. Livy, who is ill at the time, is so devastated by our son's passing that she is unable to attend his funeral in Elmira. Always the dutiful husband, I elect to stay behind with her. Tragically, my infant son goes to his grave without either of his parents being there. To make up for that omission, Livy later selects locations in the cemetery that permits both of us to be buried close to him.

"After Livy and I move into our completed residence at Nook Farm, we soon find ourselves surrounded by Beechers. Harriet Beecher Stowe known as 'Hattie,' the author of *Uncle Tom's Cabin* lives there as do two of her sisters, Mary Beecher Perkins, and Isabella Beecher Hooker. Livy and I are delighted to meet them. Many a U.S. citizen had said that with *Uncle Tom's Cabin* Hattie Stowe singlehandedly brings on the Civil War. I'm not sure I go that far, but I'll admit that her book does cause quite a stir. When it begins to outsell the Bible in the years before the war, people begin to take notice. Because they are our friends and neighbors, Hattie and her husband Calvin are often our dinner guests, which always makes for interesting evenings what with Hattie's stories and Calvin's gentle laughter. Pensive and brilliant, Calvin, is a professor who never talks much. Wisely, he gives Hattie the floor whenever possible, and she is glad to take it. [Laughter]

"On one occasion Hattie tells us about her trip to Washington at the behest of Mary Todd Lincoln. When she meets the President, he exclaims: 'So, this is the little lady who started the Great War.' Beet-red and tongue-tied, Hattie is unable to respond. After all, the president not only knows of her book, but also speaks favorably about its contents. On another occasion, Hattie tells us about receiving a small box containing a severed ear, supposedly taken from a slave.

The package comes with a warning against further attacks on slavery. She, of course, pays no attention.

"In her later years, Hattie appears to be in excellent health due, in part, to a regimen of two one-hour walks each day, which I can observe, at least partially, from where I stand hiding behind a curtain in my upstairs bedroom window. I don't choose to join her as my practice then and now is to take my exercise acting as pallbearer for friends who have chosen exercise as their primary pursuit. [Laughter] I should add that you should be careful about reading health books. You may die of a misprint. [Laughter]

"Through Hattie, we meet her brother, Henry Ward Beecher, a preacher at Plymouth Church in Brooklyn Heights, New York. The Reverend Beecher is quite famous at the time. When President Lincoln is in town, he often takes the ferry to Brooklyn Heights just to hear Beecher preach. The sermons invariably bring tears to the President's eyes, or so I'm told. I can personally attest to Beecher's popularity as a preacher. One Sunday I discover that his church is packed to the rafters for the main event. I've heard people estimate the size of his congregation at two thousand or even three thousand souls. On that day, it seems like every blessed one of them is packed in because I must squeeze myself into a space no bigger than a spittoon. [Laughter]

"Until I hear Beecher, I'm of the view that no sinner can be saved after the first twenty minutes of a sermon. With him, though, I can accept an additional five minutes or even ten minutes and hope for more. His preaching is that good. Most ministers will stay rooted to one spot behind the pulpit. Not so with Beecher who is known to roam the chancel like a hungry badger, gesticulating wildly, sometimes stopping dead in his tracks to wipe away tears. I find him to be a creature of words, big words mostly, fine words, grand words, rumbling, thundering, reverberating words with sense attached if it could be got in without marring the sound, but not otherwise. [Laughter]

"These antics are well received by his supporters who sit in wonderment until the sermon is fully hatched. He preaches a doctrine known as the Gospel of Love, which is a far cry from the doomsday predictions coming out of most churches at the time. As a result, Beecher's congregation keeps growing and growing until Plymouth Church becomes one of the biggest in the nation. When a parishioner brings an action against Beecher because of an alleged adulterous relationship with the congregant's wife, he beats the rap. I never admit to Livy and her Beecher cadre that I think he is guilty as hell. The repercussions from such a bold admission would be boundless.

"A lot of people incorrectly point to our home in Nook Farm near Hartford as the comfortable haven where I do most of my writing. Not so. The bulk of my writing is done over several summers at a place called Quarry Farm near Elmira, New York. It is an estate owned by my sister-in-law, Susan Crane. I've always loved Quarry Farm because a family setting like that gives a world-traveler like me a sense of permanence. As it turns out, the Beecher family influence follows us even to Elmira. Thomas K. Beecher, one of Hattie's brothers, becomes the minister at Park Church located there. In that position, he marries us with the assistance of Joseph Twitchell, our Pastor from Hartford. That we would uncover a Beecher connection as far away as Elmira is not surprising. Lyman Beecher, the Patriarch, spawns several sons (William, Edward, George, Henry, Charles, Thomas, and James), all of whom follow him into the ministry. With so many Beechers in so many pulpits, one can count on running into one or more of them on any given Sunday. [Laughter]

"Enough about ministers.

"To accommodate my writing while in Elmira during the summers, Susan Crane, my sister-in-law, with the help of a local carpenter, builds for me a small octagonal structure, free-standing, which is designed to look like a pilothouse, of all things. She has it placed atop a hill some distance from the main house, a location that is quiet and peaceful with a view of the valley and the Chemung River in the distance. She has a window placed in each of the eight sides to give me the ability to view the countryside from all angles. I often wonder whether part of my sister-in-law's motivation in putting me out there is to keep my cigars out of range. [Laughter] In those days I must admit that my writing practices are most unpleasant for those around me. I often smoke as many as forty cigars in a day. Even so, I consistently apply certain rules: I never smoke more than one cigar at a time, and I never smoke while sleeping. [Laughter] Livy tries several times to get me to give up this perversion, but all attempts fall flat.

Because of my love of cats, my daughter-in-law directs the builder to add a small entry-port in each of the eight sides of my octagonal study so that the little rascals can join me when they see fit. Some use the litter boxes beside the fireplace, and some don't. What with the cigar smoke and the cat smell, you can imagine what it's like in there? Cats can teach us a lot, but we should be careful to get out of an experience only the wisdom that is in it and stop there; lest we be like the cat that sits down on a hot stove-lid. She would never again sit down on a hot stove-lid, and that is well; but she will never sit down on a cold one either. [Laughter]

"Immune to the smoke and the odor, I commence my writing early each day and finish at five or so when I bring the completed pages to the front porch of the main house for a reading. The sessions involve the entire family. As you might expect, it is a command performance. My captive audience is attentive and squirms rarely. They are aware, of course, that to do otherwise would meet with a stiff rebuke. My single-mindedness about writing at Quarry Farm certainly pays off. While there, I make headway on several novels including TOM SAWYER, LIFE ON THE MISSISSIPPI, HUCKLEBERRY FINN, and THE PRINCE AND THE PAUPER.

"My family loves Quarry Farm so much that if a conflicting social invitation comes up in the summer, we always send our regrets. This practice causes me to miss Hattie Stowe's Garden Party scheduled in July of 1882 to celebrate her seventy-first birthday. When I learn later five or more poems are read in her honor that day, I'm doubly glad I'm not there. If there's anything I can't stand—even more than a Wagnerian opera—it's a poetry reading that involves lengthy and poorly-written 'poetic masterpieces.' By the way, after several years of listening, I've come to admit finally that Wagner's compositions are much better than they sound. [Laughter]

"The years go by quite swiftly. Soon enough I'm sporting bushy grey eyebrows along with my grey mane, clear evidence that old age has set in. The transition gives me quite a jolt since I feel as young as I ever did. Livy calls me 'Youth' and Livy is never wrong. However, mirrors don't lie. I'm scarified, severely cut, even flayed, each time I pass one. [Laughter] My summers at Quarry Farm are wonderful, but the good times don't last. Right off, I should admit to you that I'm not the best businessman who ever came down the pike. For example, I become convinced that the telephone is a passing fad that will never catch on. I'm reminded of my poor judgment each time I see a certain neighbor of mine who does invest come by in carriages that keep getting longer and longer and fancier and fancier. [Laughter]

"As many of you may know, I'm able to claim some experience in the printing business, so when I get word of a device being designed to set type automatically, I conclude right off that it would be a sure-fire way to make a fortune. The only trouble is that the blasted device doesn't work, a shortcoming I fail to discover until I've sunk so much money into the venture that I'm facing bankruptcy. I soon figure out that the only way to get myself out of my fix is to go on a lecture tour in Europe, which I do. Oh, we could probably have gotten by if we never bought anything or ate anything, but that doesn't seem likely. At the same time, living on a budget is a seismic shift for us, but it had to be done.

"From one standpoint, the tour is a great success because it gets the Clemens family out of debt. In another sense, the tour has certain tragic consequences. While in Europe, we receive shocking news about our eldest daughter, Susy. In our absence, while staying with the Cranes in Elmira she decides to visit our home in Nook Farm.

Somehow, she contracts spinal meningitis, and the prognosis isn't good. Intent on being available to care for Susy, Livy, and Clara, my second oldest daughter, sail for home. The telegram announcing Susy's death comes when they are halfway across the Atlantic. I hit bottom when I receive the news. The mirror in the stateroom of the ship that is bringing me home tells the tale. Whereas before receiving the news my eyes are sparkling and bright, they are now dull joyless pools splotched into a face that is pinched and pale. Susy dies at the age of twenty-four on August 18, 1896, after drifting into a coma from which she never emerges.

"The news is shattering. Worst of all, I can't get free of the memories. It's like picking at a scab until it bleeds. Poor Livy is so distraught at the loss that she vows never again to set foot in Nook Farm or Quarry Farm. She feels that the memories in both places are too vivid, and, of course, I comply with her wishes. We become nomads.

"If you'll permit me, I'd like to end on a happier note.

"Always remember that familiarity breeds contempt . . . and children. Never hope for more than one child. Twins amount to a permanent riot, and there isn't any real difference between triplets and an insurrection. I'm reminded of a story I heard recently. While the hostess is in the kitchen, her young daughter stays in the living room, entertaining the guests. One guest whispers, 'She certainly is u-g-l-y.' The child responds, 'I may be u-g-l-y, but I'm also s-m-a-r-t.'" [Laughter]

"While I'm out west, we have a real shakeup. A rumor spreads through the mining camp that one of the bartenders has fallen over a precipice to his death. The rumor proves to be an exaggeration . . . turns out he's only a chaplain. When I think back on my travels. I'm always glad I never go to Texas where they think Hanukkah is a type of bird call. [Laughter] Not that I'm serious about one faith or another . . . oh mercy no. Saint Peter recently takes a young sprout on a tour of Heaven. While passing one of the rooms, Saint Peter tells the youth to be especially quiet. 'That room is full of Catholics,' he said. 'They think they're the only ones up here.' [Laughter]

"Let me add here that that there is no distinctly criminal class except Congress. Its members with the help of the President have given us a foreign policy that is slapdash. It reminds me of the traveler confronted by a snarling pit bull, who keeps saying, 'nice, dogie, nice dogie' as he reaches for a rock. The U.S. is like the guy in the party who gives a free bottle of booze to every person at the party, and they still hate him. [Laughter]

"I have a friend who is told that the only way to keep his health is to eat what he doesn't want, drink what he doesn't like, and do what he'd rather not do. He is in perfect health right up to the day he shoots himself. Speaking of health and fitness, I may appear to be fit as a fiddle, but my doctor tells me I'm legally dead. They've discontinued my blood type. Well, not totally dead. For the record, I'd rather go to bed with Lillian Russell stark naked than Ulysses S. Grant in full military regalia. [Laughter]

"There is a lot of talk these days about drinking. Sometimes too much to drink is barely enough. Keep in mind that an alcoholic is someone you don't like who drinks as much as you do. In the same vein remember that a banker is a person who lends you an umbrella when the sun is shing and wants it back the minute it begins to rain. Late in life I've reached the conclusion that we all perform in the same way the moon does. We are determined to hide the dark side from the rest of the world. [Laughter]

"Well, that's about all I'm prepared to say . . . at least on this occasion. I want to thank you all for coming."

With that, Stephen turned and moved stage right while waving one hand to acknowledge the thunderous applause.

EPILOGUE

For Stephen and Stephanie there was time to do extensive travelling—France, Spain, Germany, England, Israel, and the Middle East. Stephanie died quietly in her sleep and Stephen followed one year later. Their assets were divided between their church and the various schools they both had attended. Stephen's peaceful demise stands in stark contrast to the terrible deaths caused by suicide that had plagued the literary ranks for so many years principally due to psychological problems including bipolar disease—writers, poets, artists, and composers over the centuries such as Ernest Hemingway, Hart Crane, Randall Jarrell, Eugene O'Neill, Sylvia Plath, Anne Sexton, Robert Schumann, Vincent van Gogh, and Virginia Woolf. Tragically, some or all might had been saved with proper treatment and appropriate medication.

AUTHOR'S NOTE

As the reader may have surmised, my interest in bipolar disease stems from my own experience. My own bipolar condition provides me insight that has enabled me to describe accurately the plight suffered by Seth Shaw and his son Brian, two of the primary characters in the novel. Despite those parallels, all the characters in this novel are fictional, or loosely based on someone real. Mark Twain's witticisms are his and not my own.

Soapy Smith was a real character. But whether he suffered from bipolar disorder in 1896 is another question. Without an appropriate diagnosis taken in a timely fashion, there is no way to know for sure. For the sake of the story, I take the position that he was a bipolar victim at the time, an assessment that gives me the opportunity as the author to speculate about the effect of that condition upon his imaginary progeny, given the disorder's well-recognized genetic component. As fictional characters, Shorty, Libby, Seth, Brian, and Stephen aren't tied in any way to real persons or events. The romantic liaison between Soapy and Libby, of course, never occurred.

I'm able to describe Seth's experience with some accuracy because I have had similar symptoms over the years. Diane, my deceased wife, being in the late stages of ovarian cancer, had been in favor of a trip to Eleuthera in the Bahamas recommended by her obstetrician. The winter weather and other complications made a motel stay near the airport mandatory the night before our morning flight. Too soon, I discovered that I'd forgotten my eyeglasses, an omission that required a round trip of several miles to our residence in bad weather. As I returned to the motel, the warmth of the car heater caused me to doze off. Abruptly, what felt like an invisible hand from the empty back seat, began shaking my shoulder.

I awoke to find the car hurtling toward a vehicle abandoned at the side of the road. I avoided a fiery crash by turning the steering wheel at the last moment. Diane told me later that my guardian angel must have intervened. Angel or not, I concluded that whatever saved me from certain death was heaven-sent. My renewed commitment to Christ occurred soon after. Seth after Rivolis makes a similar commitment.

Another personal incident that has affected my authorship took place following Diane's cancer surgery when a condition known as *shock lung* necessitated the application of a ventilator. The prognosis was bleak. We were told that unless the lungs restabilized quickly she would die. Meanwhile, Diane encountered a near-death experience while on the ventilator in which she is transported in what appeared to be an opaque tube, "much like a blood vessel," she said. A short distance ahead she saw a bright light that she recognized as a source of solace and peace. As she fell toward that light, she heard a voice say, "Diane, you must make up your mind." She responded by indicating that she didn't want to make up her mind, at which point her father's voice intervened with the same directive, causing her to reconsider. Her lung condition abruptly cleared, and in a few days, she was discharged. Eventually, however, the cancer entered her bloodstream with disastrous results. Because of that experience, the discussions in the narrative of near-death experiences (NDE's) hit home.

ACKNOWLEDGMENTS

This novel wouldn't have taken shape without extensive help from others. My wife, Shannon, deserves special credit because she had to review several drafts without complaint while at the same time acting as a cheerleader devoted to the ongoing task of keeping my spirits and confidence high. Second place on the list goes to Bill Clarkson, a good friend retired in Florida with a special talent as a lay editor. My first experience with a professional editor took place when Koehler Books expressed interest in publishing the manuscript. John Koehler kept my spirits high while Joe Coccaro dug in on the editing side. Once we got past my ego, I began to recognize what a brilliant editor can do to improve the narrative. When fellow Shepherdstown residents came forward to offer support, I was delighted. A thank you goes to Mike Austin and Betty Snyder. From many different vantage points all of you help turn *Curse of the Klondike* into a labor of love.

WRITING BIOGRAPHY

Rick's first writing efforts were directed at poetry. *Never Alone in a Cemetery* is his first self-published book, then follows *Headstone in the Headlights* and *Musings Under a Buckboard*. Although enthusiastic about his poetry, he never stopped writing fictional manuscripts and short stories. *Curse of the Klondike* is his first full-fledged novel.

He is a graduate of Pitt Law School and Denison University who presently resides in Shepherdstown, West Virginia (near the battlefield of Antietam). His poetry has been featured in *Eureka* and in the *California Quarterly*. "A Time to Walk the Ocean Floor" and "As Large as the Universe" appeared in Volume 25, Number 2 (2006) of *Westview*, a publication of Southwestern Oklahoma State University. In November of 2005 "Foxfire" was awarded third place in the 2005 Penn Writers Poetry Contest. On January 2, 2010, his poem entitled "Never Alone in the Cemetery" appeared in the *Pittsburgh Post-Gazette*. Several of his poems were recently published in *Good News*, a local Shepherdstown newspaper. *Never Alone in a Cemetery* was first on the fiction best seller list tallied by Four Seasons Bookstore in Shepherdstown for 2018. Copies of all three books can be purchased at any local bookstore or on Amazon. *Curse of the Klondike* is his first full-length novel. It, too, is available on Amazon.

*SUGGESTED READING LIST

Backhouse, Francis. *Women of the Klondike.* Vancouver/Toronto: Whitecap. 1995.

Berton, Pierre. *The Klondike Fever: The Life and Death of the Last Gold Rush.* New York: Carroll & Graf. 1958.

Byrne, Robert, Ed. *1,911 Best Things Anybody Ever Said.* New York: Ballentine. 1988.

Emerson, Everett. *The Authentic Mark Twain: A Literary Biography of Samuel L. Clemens.* Philadelphia: University of Pennsylvania Press. 1985.

Fisher, Ardis and Holmes, Opal Laurel. *Gold Rushes and Mining Camps of the Early American West.* Idaho: Claxton Printers.1979.

Jamison, Kay Redfield. *Touched With Fire.* New York: Simon & Schuster. 1993.

Jerome, Robert D. and Wisbey, Herbert A., Jr. Ed. *Mark Twain in Elmira.* New York: Mark Twain Society. 1977.

Jovanovic, Pierre. *An Inquiry into the Existence of Guardian Angels.* New York: M. Evans and Company. 1993.

Lewis, Edward and Myers, Robert, Ed. *A Treasury of Mark Twain: The Greatest Humor of the Great American Humorist.*
—Kansas City: Hallmark. 1967.

London, Jack. *Tales of the Klondike [sic].* eBook. Streetlib Write (http//write.streetlib.com).

Lynch, Jeremiah, Dale L. Morgan, Ed. *Three Years in the Klondike.* Chicago: The Lakeside Press, R. R. Donnelley & Sons. 1967.

Miller, Mark D. and Reynolds, Charles F., III. *Living Longer Depression Free: A Family Guide to Recognizing, Treating, and Preventing Depression in Later Life.* Baltimore: Johns Hopkins.2002.

Morrow, Pat and Hume, Andrew. *The Yukon.* Vancouver: Whitecap Books. 1979.

Perry, Mark. *Grant and Twain.* New York: Random House. 2004.

Powers, Ron. *Mark Twain: A Life.* New York: Free Press.2005

Rasmussen, R. Kent. *Mark Twain A-Z: The Essential Reference to His Life and Writings.* New York: Oxford. 1995.

Seagraves, Anne. *Soiled Doves: Prostitution in the Early West.* Hayden Idaho: Wesanne. 1994.

Service, Robert William. *Best Tales of the Yukon.* Philadelphia: Running Press. 1983.

Schoenbrun, David. *Soldiers of the Night: The Story of the French Resistance.* New York: E.P. Dutton. 1980.

Taylor, Rick. *Never Alone in a Cemetery.* Shepherdstown: Cezno Press/Ingram Spark. 2017.

— *Headstone in the Headlights.* Shepherdstown: Cezno Press/ Ingram Spark. 2018.

—*Musings Under a Buckboard.* Shepherdstown: Cezno Press/ Ingram Spark. 2019.

Winchester, Simon. *A Crack at the Edge of the World: America and the Great California Earthquake of 1906.* New York: —2005.

CPSIA information can be obtained
at www.ICGtesting.com
Printed in the USA
LVHW110015021122
732111LV00004B/117

9 781646 638147